# Birthd

## *Sage Gardens Cozy Mystery Series*

**Cindy Bell**

**Copyright © 2015 Cindy Bell**

**All rights reserved.**

ISBN-13: 978-1508612339

ISBN-10: 1508612331

# More Cozy Mysteries by Cindy Bell

## Dune House Cozy Mysteries

Seaside Secrets

Boats and Bad Guys

Treasured History

Hidden Hideaways

Dodgy Dealings

## Heavenly Highland Inn Cozy Mysteries

Murdering the Roses

Dead in the Daisies

Killing the Carnations

Drowning the Daffodils

Suffocating the Sunflowers

Books, Bullets and Blooms

A Deadly serious Gardening Contest

A Bridal Bouquet and a Body

## Wendy the Wedding Planner Cozy Mysteries

Matrimony, Money and Murder

Chefs, Ceremonies and Crimes

Knives and Nuptials

## Bekki the Beautician Cozy Mysteries

Hairspray and Homicide

A Dyed Blonde and a Dead Body

Mascara and Murder

Pageant and Poison

Conditioner and a Corpse

Mistletoe, Makeup and Murder

Hairpin, Hair Dryer and Homicide

Blush, a Bride and a Body

Shampoo and a Stiff

Cosmetics, a Cruise and a Killer

Lipstick, a Long Iron and Lifeless

Camping, Concealer and Criminals

# Table of Contents

Chapter One ........................................... 1

Chapter Two ......................................... 19

Chapter Three ......................................29

Chapter Four ........................................43

Chapter Five ........................................55

Chapter Six ..........................................63

Chapter Seven ................................... 80

Chapter Eight .....................................97

Chapter Nine ......................................114

Chapter Ten........................................ 132

Chapter Eleven ................................. 156

Chapter Twelve................................... 170

Chapter Thirteen .............................189

Chapter Fourteen ......................... 205

Chapter Fifteen ................................................. 217

Chapter Sixteen ............................................... 239

Chapter Seventeen .......................................... 248

Chapter Eighteen ............................................ 259

# Chapter One

A bright orange balloon floated just above the multitude of tiny, green leaves on the tall hedges that surrounded Sage Gardens. Outside the hedges the busy streets were filled with people rushing to get home from work, but inside the hedges, the community was populated by people who no longer had to participate in rush hour. Sage Gardens was a retirement community that welcomed anyone over the age of sixty-five. It was normally a rather quiet environment, but this bright, spring day it was quite active. The manicured grounds were busy with people headed for the recreation hall which stood at the end of a long cobblestone walkway. Eddy's dark blue eyes narrowed as he watched the parade of residents walk past him. They seemed to be following the man with the balloon. Each dressed in a brighter button-down than the last.

"These people must think this is Hawaii," he

muttered to himself and rolled his eyes. He tugged his gray fedora down a little tighter over his thinning, brown hair. He was dressed as always in a simple, light brown suit. It was what he had worn for years when he worked as a detective, and it was what he continued to wear, even though he was now retired and living in Sage Gardens.

Sage Gardens stressed independence while providing a safe environment for people to enjoy. Eddy found it to be rather boring, but he could appreciate having staff on hand to help with things he would rather not do, such as mowing the lawn, or repairing the roof. Several things about Sage Gardens annoyed Eddy. Whenever there was a special event, the residents acted as if it was the party of the century. Today it was a birthday party for one of the residents, James. Eddy didn't know James very well. He kept himself at a distance from most people, and enjoyed his time alone.

"Isn't it exciting?" a voice chirped from just behind him. He closed his eyes briefly and clenched his jaw. He knew that voice very well.

"Hello, Samantha," he said as he turned to face her. She was wearing the brightest pink button-down shirt he had ever seen, and he had watched the entire parade walk past. Her copper-red hair was peppered with a few gray strands here and there. She wore it long and almost always had it back in a tight braid. Her bright green eyes were shining as they met his.

"Aren't you going to the party, Eddy?" she asked and swept her gaze across his drab suit.

"Sure," he shrugged and reached up to tug at the brim of his hat. "If there's going to be cake then I'll be there."

"I love birthday parties," Samantha said happily and draped her arm through his. He was a little startled by the gesture but didn't bother to fight it. Ever since Samantha had arrived at Sage Gardens she had made it her mission to cheer Eddy up a little bit. Eddy didn't want to be cheered up. He was perfectly content with things as they were. But he found that if he resisted Samantha it only made her more determined. If he allowed himself to be swept up in her happy thought of the day, then she was appeased, and he could go back to being practically isolated.

"What is the point of birthday parties at this age?" Eddy demanded as they began walking towards the recreation hall.

"What do you mean?" Samantha asked as she glanced over at him. "Don't you ever want to celebrate?"

"Sure, if it's worth celebrating," he replied mildly. "I mean, what's to celebrate about getting another year older. After sixty, it's kind of pointless, don't you think? Happy birthday, you lost more hair! Happy birthday, you're going to need to go on a special diet to lower your cholesterol!"

"Oh, Eddy," Samantha rolled her eyes. "You just need to relax and enjoy yourself."

"I said that I would eat cake," Eddy pointed out.

When they reached the door of the recreation

hall, Samantha politely withdrew her arm from his. One thing the residents did at Sage Gardens was gossip. She was looking forward to spending some time, singing, laughing, and dancing. Samantha loved any break from routine, and anything that would pull her away from the endless articles she intended to write. She had retired from her career as a journalist, but every time that she had an idea about something to write she jotted it down in her notebook. As a result she had over one hundred articles that were waiting to be written. However, she had only managed a few words on each one. Though she loved to write she found that getting started was one of the hardest parts.

Eddy opened the tall metal door for her and she stepped inside. As usual the recreation hall had been decorated for the birthday party. There was a party committee that took care of these things. Samantha had tried to sign up for it, but the group of women who ran it were very snooty and didn't seem to enjoy new people. She had to admit, the ladies did an excellent job with their ribbons, banners, and balloons, although it struck her as a little childish. The tables were still being set up for the party. James, the birthday man himself was standing near one of the longer, folding tables. Beside him, a younger man was setting a sheet cake down on the table.

"Here's your cupcake, Dad," Mike said and handed James a small, white box. "I had them make it special, and it is completely gluten free, so you don't have to worry about eating it."

"Wonderful," James nodded with a broad smile as he looked at his son. "Thank you so much, Mike."

"Anything for your birthday, Dad," Mike said and smiled back at his father. The two mirrored each other well. They both had straight, black hair, though James' was receding to the point of revealing most of his scalp. They both had clear blue eyes that reminded Samantha of the ocean in the morning. They were about the same height, but Mike was at least thirty pounds heavier, with most of it being in his middle. James took his health very seriously. Samantha always spotted him in the on-site gym or out for a jog around the large lake that the individual villas were centered around. Samantha admired him for it, as she found it hard to stick to a healthy lifestyle herself.

"Well, the wolves are here," Eddy commented as he stepped in behind her and glanced over the people that had already collected in the recreation hall. Samantha didn't have to ask to know who he was talking about. There were several self-declared bachelors that lived in Sage Gardens and they were always on the hunt. Samantha did her best to avoid them.

Eddy walked over to the punch bowl to get himself a drink. He preferred to blend into the scenery at parties, but he did enjoy the free food.

"Check the cake, Dad, and make sure that the inscription is right," Mike said with a sly smile. James eyed him closely.

"Did you have them write something mean?" he asked suspiciously.

"Just check it," Mike insisted impatiently.

James turned towards the cake and was about to open the lid to check the inscription when he suddenly froze. He was looking in the direction of the entrance of the recreation hall. A man stood in the doorway. Samantha didn't recognize him, but she did notice the way that he stared straight across the room at James. The two men locked eyes with enough tension to make the hairs on the back of Samantha's neck stand up. Eddy paused beside the punch bowl and spared a glance in the direction of the two men.

"Frank," James said as he stared at the man. His skin had grown pale and his smile had faded from his lips.

"James," Frank replied in a cool voice and took a slight step forward. James walked around the table towards Frank.

"Listen Frank, I'm sorry," James said in one breath. "I've been wanting to apologize."

"No need," Frank said sternly and smoothed the lapel of his suit jacket. It was black and tailored to fit him. His pants matched it. His silver hair was nearly the same shade as the shirt he wore under his suit jacket. "What's in the past, is in the past, James," he held his hand out in front of him in a friendly manner. James appeared a little shocked as he studied the man before him. Then he raised his own hand and took Frank's. The two men shook hands, and then let their hands fall back to their sides. James lingered for a moment longer as if he didn't quite know what to say.

"Nice party," Frank commented quietly. He nodded his head towards the others nearby, then he turned and walked towards a table of refreshments. Samantha was curious about him, as he was not a face she knew. She wondered if he was a close friend of James'. She made her way over to the refreshment table and picked up a small, paper plate. She smiled at the decorative balloon shapes on the plate. She always tried to appreciate the little things. She stood close to Frank as she picked through the food.

"Hi, I'm Sam," she said casually as she glanced over at him. He seemed a little startled that she had spoken to him. He managed a small smile that barely altered his hardened expression. His light green eyes were narrowed. Samantha could sense the tension that filled him.

"Frank," he replied. "I'm new here. Just moved in."

"Oh really?" Samantha asked with surprise. "You must have taken Baki's old place," she said as a warm smile arose on her lips. "We're practically neighbors."

"Is that so?" he chuckled in a friendly way. "Well, it's good to meet you, neighbor," he said. "If you'll excuse me, I think I forgot something in my villa," he stepped away from her carrying his plate of food. Samantha watched him go. She wondered if he was trying to avoid her or if he had really forgotten something. Either way she didn't care too much. If he didn't want to be friends, she was okay with that. But she had to know who he was and what he was doing at Sage Gardens. Now that she did, she felt a little calmer. Her curiosity always got her wrapped up in things she shouldn't be, but she couldn't ignore it. If she wanted to know about something or someone, she had to get to the bottom of it before she could feel settled.

"Did you get the scoop?" Eddy asked as he picked up his own paper plate and began to scope out the food.

"New resident," Samantha explained. "He moved into Baki's old place."

"Oh boy, I hope he didn't leave any of his rabbit's feet behind," Eddy said with genuine laughter. "Baki hid them everywhere."

"I guess Frank will find them soon enough if he did," Samantha laughed as well.

"Excuse me for a few minutes, Mike," James said to his son as he stepped away from the table. "I'm just going to get something I left in my room."

"Can I get it for you?" Mike offered.

"No, it's fine, I'll get it," James said and waved

his hand as he walked away.

"Well, don't be long, we'll be doing the cake soon," Mike reminded him.

"I'll be back quickly," James assured him.

Eddy heard the clang of the door closing and glanced up to see Walt walking through the chairs that were set up in the middle of the room. The tall and slender man was dotting a finger lightly on the back of each chair. Eddy knew him well enough from observing him to know exactly what he was doing, he was counting all of the chairs. Walt was a retired accountant and he kept track of everything. His silver, thin-framed glasses were always perched perfectly on the bridge of his nose. He always paired sweaters with pleated pants and wore the same polished brown shoes.

"Walt, over here," Eddy said and waved his hand to the only resident, besides Samantha, he would consider more than just an acquaintance at Sage Gardens. Walt looked up at Eddy and offered him a friendly smile.

"Hi Eddy, I was wondering if you would be

here," he said as he walked over to Eddy. Eddy nodded and tilted his head towards the food.

"Anywhere there is free food, you'll find me," he said with a chuckle.

"Looks like a good spread," Walt nodded his approval.

"Grab a plate," Eddy encouraged him. "They're getting the party started when James comes back."

"All right," Walt said and carefully picked up a plate. He dusted it lightly with his fingertips to ensure that there were no crumbs already on it. Then he began methodically selecting certain foods to place on his plate.

By the time Walt had his plate piled high with food James had returned and everyone had begun to gather around the long table to sing happy birthday and get some cake.

Walt walked over to join in, but Eddy hung back. He preferred to be an observer in these kinds of situations.

"Are you coming?" Walt asked as he glanced over his shoulder.

"Nah, I'm fine here. But get me a piece of cake," he requested.

"I don't know if I can do that," Walt said. "It's one piece of cake per person, and I'm one person. If I take two, then people will think I'm taking too much and..."

"Never mind," Eddy waved his hand. "I'll get my own cake," he followed Walt over to the group. As he hung back from the crowd Samantha stepped up beside him. She looked a little troubled as she shot a scowl in the direction of Naomi, one of the women who was on the decorating committee.

"Not so chipper?" Eddy asked as he glanced over at her.

"Drop it," Samantha insisted and plastered a smile on her face as she turned to face James.

It wasn't long before the entire group had joined in on singing the Happy Birthday song to

James. James cheered in response and leaned forward to blow out the numerous candles on his cake. Everyone clapped to celebrate James' monumental achievement of making it through another year. As Mike cut the cake and began handing out plates to everyone, Samantha frowned.

"Shouldn't James get the first piece?" she asked politely.

"He has his own cupcake," Mike explained. "Dad's gluten intolerant."

"Oh, that's right," Samantha nodded a little and smiled warmly at Mike. "It was so nice of you to put all of this together for him."

"It was the least I could do," Mike offered a polite smile in return. He handed her a piece of cake, which she accepted.

"Everyone, attention everyone," Mike said as he tapped his glass lightly with a fork creating a light clinking sound. It did get the attention of most of the people in the room, who turned to look at him. He raised his glass in the air. "I'd like to offer a toast to my father on his birthday," he explained and turned to face his father.

James smiled sheepishly and looked up at his son fondly. "That's not necessary," he said dismissively.

"I want to," Mike said firmly. "I have a lot to say actually. You see, my father and I, we didn't always get along. A father son rift, who would have thought?" he laughed. A few people around him laughed as well. "Anyway, all of that is in the past now. But when I think of all of the birthdays that I've missed it's hard for me not to feel as if I missed out on an awful lot. I missed out on the first gray hair," he cleared his throat. "Of which he now has many."

"That's not true," James laughed loudly.

"I missed out on the first trip to the dentist, where he got to leave his teeth overnight," Mike continued. His comment got a roar of laughter from the people attending the party. James balled up a napkin and tossed it playfully at his son.

"Enough!" he pleaded.

"All right, all joking aside, I feel very grateful that I will get to share this, and every birthday to come with you, Dad," he said and raised his glass to his father. James stood up from his chair and clinked his glass with his son's. He drank down the champagne that had been provided for the party.

"Thank you, Son," he said and clapped Mike firmly on the back. "You've grown to be a fine man. I'm very proud of you."

"Thank you, Dad," Mike smiled. When James sat back down at the table Samantha watched him pour himself a glass of wine and then tuck the bottle under the table by his side where his gifts were. There was plenty of champagne and other bottles of wine to drink.

Samantha helped herself to a glass of white. She was enjoying the festivities of the party. If there was one thing she felt she did right in her life it was moving to Sage Gardens. She felt secure, and there were plenty of people for her to spend time with. She hadn't quite broken into the social scene yet, but she knew with a little patience she soon would.

As Samantha walked off to talk to one of the women on the decorating committee, a gasp began to carry through the crowd. She spun around in time to see James standing up behind the table. He was clutching his chest. His eyes were wide and he looked hungry for air. He reached for his son, but before he could get a grasp on Mike's hand he collapsed and slumped down across the table.

# Chapter Two

"Dad?" Mike cried out as he leaned towards his father. The nurse who worked in the community rushed forward to check on James.

"Is he okay, Owen?" Samantha gasped as she watched the nurse attempt to rouse James. Others nearby tried to gather close to check on him, but Owen waved them away.

"Give him space," he demanded, his voice troubled. "Call for an ambulance, quickly," he shouted.

Owen pulled James off the table and spread him out on the floor. He began doing chest compressions while the nurse's aide called for an ambulance. Mike, still in a daze, stared down at his father sprawled across the floor.

"All right, everyone, the party is over," the nurse's aide said, after she had hung up, and began waving the guests towards the door of the recreation hall. "Let's give James some privacy," she pleaded with the stragglers.

As everyone began to leave, Samantha did her best to linger. She wanted to know whether James was going to make it. Soon, she was one of the only people remaining in the hall. She noticed that Eddy was also still in the hall, standing near the exit. He noticed her as well, before shifting his gaze back towards Owen.

"Dad," Mike said as he crouched down beside his father. "Please wake up."

Samantha looked at James thinking that it did not look as if there was much chance of him waking up. Eddy opened the door for the paramedics who rushed in with a gurney in tow.

"I don't think James is going to make it," Eddy said quietly to Samantha.

"Don't say that," Samantha argued in a whisper, though she knew that he was right. "He could still pull through, we just have to think positively about it."

"Okay, you go on and think positive about it,"

Eddy said with a hint of animosity. He got a little fed up with the positive thought movement.

Owen stepped away from James and let the paramedics take over. He looked up to see Samantha and Eddy still in the recreation hall.

"Guys, you really need to clear out," Owen said gravely. Samantha noticed that he refused to look directly at her. She nodded her head.

"Sorry, Owen, I just wanted to see if there was any way that I could help."

"The paramedics are handling it," Owen said, though his voice wavered when he spoke. Owen was a very caring nurse. He didn't just do his job, he seemed to care about the people that he worked with. He was also studying to become a doctor. Samantha thought he would be a great one since he was genuinely invested in the well-being of his patients.

As Eddy and Samantha were turning towards the door, one of the paramedics walked over to Owen and spoke quietly to him. When Owen looked over at Eddy and Samantha he didn't have to say anything for them to realize that James had passed away, his face said it all.

Eddy opened the door for Samantha and they stepped out of the recreation hall.

As the door clanged shut behind him, Eddy grimaced. He looked over at Samantha.

"It's so sad," Samantha said quietly. "To die at your birthday party."

"I know, it's terrible," Eddy said looking at the ground.

"Are you coming?" Samantha asked.

"I'm just going to wait here a bit longer," Eddy replied.

"All right," Samantha nodded. She watched him for a moment as if she was about to ask him a question, but instead she turned and walked away. Eddy surveyed the flood of brightly colored shirts heading back to the villas that wrapped around the lake in nearly a full circle. The further away they got, the more they looked like the cheerful birthday balloons that the recreation hall was dotted with.

"Easy come, easy go," he muttered to himself and shook his head at the demise of the celebration. Soon, he was the only person near the recreation hall. Eddy kicked the toe of his shoe lightly against the sandy dirt that surrounded the front steps. He pretended to be searching for something in the dirt. He would come up with what he was searching for if anyone asked him what he was up to. The door opened and Owen stepped outside.

"Owen," Eddy said in a cool tone and offered him a nod.

"Eddy, not surprised to find you here," he said grimly as he locked eyes with Eddy.

"I think I dropped something," Eddy muttered and kicked at the dirt again.

"Nice try, Eddy," Owen shook his head and descended the steps to join him. "I know why you're here."

"So?" Eddy asked. "What really happened in

there?" he knew that Owen would tell him everything there was to tell. Owen was fascinated by the cop stories that Eddy would share with him. Most of them true. Some were slightly embellished because it amused Eddy to see Owen so interested. Of all the people at Sage Gardens, Eddy felt the most comfortable around Owen.

"It looks like a heart attack," Owen said quietly and then tilted his head towards the corner of the building. The two men walked around the side of the building. Eddy studied Owen curiously. Owen lowered his voice. "He had a strange rash on his skin and his skin was so pink, Eddy. I've never seen anything like it before and certainly never heard of anything like that occurring with a heart attack."

"What are you saying, Owen?" Eddy asked as he narrowed his eyes.

"I'm not saying anything really," Owen replied nervously and glanced over his shoulder. "I'm only telling you because of your history, Eddy. I just don't feel right about calling this a simple heart attack."

"What do you think it was?" Eddy pressed sternly. He knew how to get a confession out of just about anyone.

"I'm not sure," Owen admitted hesitantly. "If I had to guess, I would say that he had a strong reaction to something that caused a heart attack. Maybe medication or even poison. "

"Poison," Eddy repeated as he mulled over the possibility. "Some poisons can cause symptoms like a heart attack," he agreed slowly.

"So, you think I might be right?" Owen asked with a hint of excitement at the idea of seeing through a crime.

"Hmm," Eddy rubbed his hands together twice. "To tell you the truth, Owen, as a detective I always relied more on the why than the how."

"What is the why?" Owen asked, his brow furrowed.

"It is the motive. Okay, we know James is dead. We know he could have possibly died from a heart attack, or he could have possibly been poisoned with something that would make it look like natural causes. So, the quick question that comes to mind is, who would want James dead? Who would go to the lengths of poisoning him? If you can find a reason, or a person in his life that might be the driving force behind his death, then I would be more likely to move towards poison. However, that is sometimes a hard thing to prove."

"Do you think that it's possible?" Owen asked. "James was fairly well off. I imagine the only person who stood to gain from his death was his son."

"So, maybe his son didn't want to wait any longer for the old man to get sick and die. With James being in such good health, maybe he was just getting impatient to get his hands on his inheritance."

"I'd hate to think that, but I guess it is possible," Owen said quietly.

"No one wants to think it, but clearly it's a

possibility," Eddy said. "Let me know what the medical examiner says, okay?"

"Sure," Owen nodded and then lowered his voice. "I've never seen an actual murder victim before," he admitted nervously.

"And you probably haven't now," Eddy reminded him. "We don't have any idea what this is yet. Jumping to conclusions won't solve anything."

"You're right," Owen said and ruffled his hand back through his hair. "I guess I got caught up in the idea."

"I'm not saying you're wrong, Owen," Eddy reminded him sternly. "You have good instincts. But until we get some kind of proof we won't know for sure."

"Hopefully they'll run a tox screen. But even if they do it will probably take a while to get the results," Owen said grimly. "I guess we'll just have to wait and see."

"Maybe," Eddy replied thoughtfully. "Keep

me informed, all right?"

"Sure, of course I will," Owen nodded. "I better check on a few of the residents that were at the party today. It had to be a shocking experience for everyone."

Eddy nodded as Owen walked away from him. He looked back towards the recreation hall and felt a bit excited at the prospect of investigating a murder. He had been retired for years. It had been a very long time since he was involved in an actual murder investigation. He had tracked down killers for a living, and he was not about to let a murder go unpunished, especially one that happened right under his nose.

# Chapter Three

As Samantha was walking back towards her villa, the few residents that hadn't been at the party when James collapsed were hurrying towards the sound of the sirens. The thing about a small, secure place like Sage Gardens was that if there was any sign of trouble, everybody wanted to know about it.

As she walked past a bench she decided to sit down and look over the lake so she could try to come to terms with James' passing. While she was looking at the water she was distracted by the residents that were walking away from the recreation hall as they walked past. They were looking either shocked or sad. The news of James' passing was obviously getting around Sage Gardens.

Samantha glanced down the hill at the villa that had once belonged to Baki. She and Baki had played cards on a regular basis. He used to make her Chinese tea and always had some new book to share with her. It was a cozy little place that Samantha had loved to retreat to for hours. Now it belonged to Frank, the newest resident at Sage Gardens.

Samantha was curious about Frank. She was curious about most new residents, but something about Frank had caught her attention. Something about him made her think he had some unusual experiences to share. She considered going down the hill to check things out, and perhaps introduce herself, but she was distracted by the presence of someone else. She turned to see Jo, another resident, slinking down the corridor between the villas. As usual, Jo was dressed in a sleek outfit. She had paired black, leather pants with a skin-tight, off-white top. She was also walking in the opposite direction of everyone else, which sparked Samantha's curiosity even more.

Ever since Jo had recently arrived at Sage Gardens, Samantha had been paying special attention to her. She dressed differently to most of the residents. She seemed to exude a certain sense of arrogance and confidence. But more importantly than that, she seemed familiar to Samantha. It was hard for her to place why, but Samantha felt as if she had known her at some point in her life. She could not recall ever associating with anyone that would dress the way that Jo did. Yet, every time Samantha saw her she felt like calling out to her, as if they were old friends. Samantha was caught between two curiosities, Frank the new and intriguing stranger, or Jo, the mysterious diva that she could barely get to speak a word.

As Jo disappeared around the side of one of the villas, Samantha stood up and headed in the direction of Frank's villa. He obviously knew James. If they were old friends or even just old acquaintances he might be very upset by his passing and would need some comfort. She walked down the sloping walkway towards the lake.

Frank's villa was one of the closest to the lake. All of the villas had a view of the lake, but Frank's villa was one of the few that had a small dock that stretched out into the water. Baki used to sit out on the dock and pretend to fish. He didn't even put a lure or bait on the line. He confided in Samantha that it was his way of hanging out on the dock and ensuring no one would disturb him, as everyone assumed he needed quiet in order to fish. Otherwise, if he just sat out on the dock the entire neighborhood would be outside and wanting to join him. The people of Sage Gardens did have a habit of getting into each other's business fairly frequently. Of course Samantha's interest in Frank was for much more than pure gossip. She wanted to make sure that he was okay after James' death, and that he was settling into the villa well.

When she knocked on the door of the villa she could see that the windows were dark. It was still light outside, but usually the kitchen light, or a television would be on, to indicate that someone was home. Samantha was about to walk away when she heard the door handle shake. She turned back just as the door was opening. Framed by the doorway Frank looked a bit larger and stronger than she recalled. She was startled by his sudden presence, despite the fact that she had knocked on the door expecting him to answer.

"Hi," she said nervously.

"Hello?" he replied with a hint of annoyance. "Can I help you?"

Samantha felt as if she was in the crosshairs of a weapon. She had planned out all of the things that she would say to Frank before he opened the door. Now that she was staring directly into his eyes, she couldn't recall a single thing she had planned on saying.

"I'm sorry, I'm Samantha, Sam," she explained and offered her hand for a handshake. "I met you at the party today," she added as he didn't seem to recognize her. As her hand hovered in the air before her, she realized just how awkward the situation was. Did anyone even shake hands anymore? Reluctantly, Frank reached out and shook her hand.

"Are there more of you?" he asked and leaned forward to look past her, up the hill.

"More of me?" Samantha asked with confusion. "What do you mean?"

"I mean, you're the first," Frank shrugged as he met her eyes.

"The first what?" Samantha was getting even more confused by the moment.

"The first of the single women to just show up on my door step," Frank replied impatiently. "It happens every time I move into one of these places. All of the single women smell fresh blood and decide to introduce themselves for no apparent reason. I find it extremely forward and distasteful."

Samantha swallowed thickly. She had never been so embarrassed. Her mind couldn't keep up with what he was accusing her of doing.

"Excuse me, but I had no intention of coming here to introduce myself to the fresh blood. I came here to check on you, because of what happened to James. I noticed the way you two were talking, and assumed that you might be old friends, which made me think I should make sure that you are handling the news okay," she explained. Her voice was even and confident as she spoke, but inwardly she still felt flustered by his accusations.

"What do you mean? What news?" Frank demanded, it was clear that his patience was on its last thread.

"Oh, wait, weren't you at the recreation hall?" she asked, startled once more.

"I was," he replied darkly. "You know I was, obviously. But I left. Did something happen at the party?" he narrowed his eyes.

Samantha felt her breath catch in her throat. She hadn't expected to be the one to inform Frank of his friend's death. The very idea made her uncomfortable. She glanced over her shoulder to see if anyone else was nearby that she could pass the duty onto. However, no one was anywhere near Frank's villa.

"What is this all about?" Frank demanded as

he glowered at her.

"I'm sorry to be the one to tell you this," Samantha said hesitantly. "But your friend, James, passed away today at the party. I think it was a heart attack."

"Is this some kind of sick joke?" Frank asked, his voice raising with each word. "Are you crazy enough to make something like that up just to get my attention?"

"I didn't make it up," Samantha shot back with frustration. She caught herself, and reminded herself that Frank was just in shock. "Didn't you hear the sirens?" she demanded.

"Well, I assumed they might be common around here," Frank replied with disbelief. "Are you saying it was James?"

"Yes," Samantha nodded and then frowned when she saw the shock in his eyes. "I'm very sorry for your loss."

"I can't believe this," Frank said and shook his head. "You never know when it will be your time, do you?" he asked wistfully.

"No, we never do," Samantha agreed and then reached out to lightly touch his shoulder. "I'm sorry, I thought you already knew. I just didn't want you to have to grieve all alone."

"That's very kind of you," Frank said softly as he met her eyes. "Maybe you'd like to come in for a moment?" he suggested. "I think I need to sit down."

"Sure," Samantha smiled with a touch of warmth. Now that Frank's demeanor towards her had shifted she could tell that he wasn't as tough as he portrayed himself to be. She helped him back into the villa and settled him down on the couch inside. She noticed it was still Baki's couch. She assumed Frank hadn't even had time to properly move himself in just yet. "Let me get you some water?" she suggested.

"A beer," Frank requested. "There are some in the fridge. Help yourself if you'd like one."

Samantha stepped into the tiny, familiar kitchen. She felt a pang of grief for her friend,

Baki. She loved that he was able to be close to his daughter, but she missed him. She opened the fridge to find a six pack of beer. Beside it was a pack of lunch meat and some cheese. That was the extent of Frank's food.

As she grabbed one of the beers out of the pack, she noticed that two more were missing. She wondered how much Frank drank each day. Reminding herself not to judge she turned to carry the bottle into Frank. As she did she nearly tripped on the trashcan that was sticking partially out of the cabinet. All of the villas were equipped with slide out trashcans in the kitchen to make the most of the small space. Samantha happened to know that Baki's often got stuck. It was clear that the problem hadn't been fixed before renting the villa to a new resident. She decided to fix it for Frank as he had enough to deal with. She gave the trashcan a hard tug and then slammed it back into the cabinet. Something in the trashcan clanged together. She assumed that it was the beer bottles that were missing from the six-pack. The trashcan didn't quite slide back into place. She tugged it out again and was about to slam it again, when Frank's voice interrupted her.

"Stop that!" he commanded her and rushed over towards her.

"Oh sorry, I am just fixing it for you," Samantha explained. "This one always gets stuck."

"I don't need your help," Frank growled. "I don't need your meddling either."

"Frank, I'm sorry," Samantha said quickly as she tried to meet his eyes. "I know that you must be upset about James."

"I'm upset about having my privacy invaded," he said and snatched the beer from her hand. "I just want to be left alone."

"If you say so," Samantha said hesitantly. "Are you sure there's nothing I can do for you?"

Frank stared at her without responding. She turned away from him swiftly. "I'll just be on my way then," she said.

Samantha was just about at the door when Frank called out to her. "Sam, I'm sorry," he said as he stood in the doorway of the kitchen. "I didn't mean to be so harsh. It's just, I'm going through a lot right now, and my temper gets the better of me sometimes."

"No need to apologize," Samantha said as she opened the front door and prepared to step out. "You're entitled to your feelings."

"I just need some time to settle in," Frank explained. He set his beer down on the table beside two empty bottles. "Maybe once I am, you could show me around a little?" he offered her a charming smile.

"Maybe," Samantha replied politely, then she stepped out the door. She pulled it shut behind her. As soon as she was outside she breathed a sigh of relief. She shook off the experience and tried not to let it bother her.

As she continued walking towards her villa she noticed Eddy and Owen talking by the recreation hall. That did not surprise her. Eddy and Owen were always sharing lunch or walking by the lake. Owen had a strange fascination with Eddy, and Eddy didn't seem to mind the attention, which was a little surprising, since he did his best to avoid almost everyone else.

Samantha reached her own villa and let herself in. Everything inside was decorated with light blues and teals. She liked things to be bright and airy. Since moving into Sage Gardens she had dedicated herself to a positive lifestyle. Maybe it was her way of balancing out all of the crime and gore she had written about during her career. Her mind shifted back to James' death. The only way she had to get things out that were troubling her, was to write them down. She sat down with her notebook and pen and began scribbling out what she had witnessed at the party. She always focused on the little details that were easily overlooked. She noted James' interaction with his son. She wrote about him having his own special cupcake. Then she described the scene as he collapsed on the table.

As she was finishing, she realized she hadn't noticed when Frank left the recreation hall as he claimed. She wondered if it was the same time that James had left. Maybe they had a discussion that triggered James to be more upset than his body could handle. Samantha frowned as she made this note on the paper. Then she closed up her notebook. She decided it was far past time for her to take a nap, considering the events of the day. She walked into her bedroom and sprawled out on the sea-blue shaded comforter that was stretched across her bed. She closed her eyes and imagined she was drifting off on the waves. Each wave was a pleasant thought. It was the only way she had been able to fall asleep in years.

# Chapter Four

Walt stood out front of his villa. He was carefully watering each of his plants. He liked to grow green things. He was not that fond of flowers. All of his plants had a purpose. Most were herbs, some kept pests away in the tropical climates. Usually, watering his plants was the most relaxing activity of his day, but not today. He was disturbed by the gathering around the main square of Sage Gardens. Someone had thought it would be a good idea to hold a candlelight vigil for James, since he had passed so suddenly, and on his birthday. Walt did not enjoy social things. He often avoided them. He knew that most of Sage Gardens had probably gathered for the ceremony, but he had no intention of joining them. Until Samantha came walking up.

"Walt, put down your watering can. We should show our respects," Samantha said as she paused in front of his garden.

"I'd really rather not, Samantha," Walt said

with a frown. "I didn't know James all that well, and there are a lot of people."

"Walt, you have to come out of your shell sometime," Samantha pointed out with a gentle smile. Walt always felt at ease around Samantha. She never forced him to do anything, but he always ended up doing anything that she asked. When he had first moved into Sage Gardens she brought him a basket of muffins to welcome him. He appreciated that each was individually wrapped, and there were exactly six. He liked things to be even. She had struck up a conversation and Walt had been surprised that he didn't mind her company. Instead he found it to be quite enjoyable.

"I don't actually," he smiled a little. "But, I think tonight is a good night to stay in it."

"Why?" Samantha asked with a troubled expression. "Doesn't it bother you at all?"

"Well, I don't mean to be cold, but no," he shook his head slowly.

"How can you say that?" Samantha asked, her

eyes wide. Walt frowned. He didn't enjoy confrontation, or upsetting anyone, especially Samantha.

"I said I don't mean to be cold," he reminded her. "It's just that I didn't know James very well. Is it sad? Yes. Does it bother me? No," he shook his head.

"Shouldn't it though?" Samantha pressed. "I mean, one minute we were singing happy birthday to him, and the next he was gone. Really, that could have been any of us."

Walt drew a long, slow breath. He set down his watering can and looked up at her with trepidation. "There's no need to be so morbid, Samantha," he pointed out.

"I'm not being morbid," Samantha argued as she turned away from him and looked at the gathering of people in the square. "Who do you think that vigil is really for, Walt?" she asked.

"For James," Walt pointed out with confidence.

"James isn't here anymore," Samantha said quietly. "He can't see any of this. The vigil is for the people left behind, those that are witnesses to just how fragile life is, how suddenly it can be taken from you."

Walt reached out and lightly touched Samantha's shoulder. She glanced over her shoulder and smiled at him as he looked at her sympathetically.

"You're not going anywhere yet, Sam," he said reassuringly.

"If I did, I wouldn't know it, would I?" she asked with a slight laugh. "I guess there's some comfort in that. The not knowing."

"Maybe," Walt frowned. "I've honestly never found comfort in anything but numbers. I've already figured out when I will die."

"What?" Samantha looked at him with shock. "That's not possible, Walt."

"I know, it's just an estimate," Walt explained. "But statistically and taking into account my genetic history, I estimate my death will be around the age of eighty-six."

"I hope not," Samantha grimaced. "I don't like to think about it too much. I mean, if we're lucky we'll have a long life."

"Unless you're murdered," Eddy's gruff voice said from beside the villa as he walked up to them.

"Now, who is being morbid?" Samantha shook her head.

"Oh now, there's no need to make it an emotional thing," Eddy said as he too turned to look at the gathering. "They're all up there wiping their tears and singing songs tonight, but tomorrow they'll be fighting over his favorite lounge chair by the pool."

Samantha opened her mouth to argue, but she couldn't. She knew that he was right. She had seen it happen.

"But the point is that no one knows," Samantha said and squeezed her hands together tightly before brushing off her palms, as if she was trying to rid herself of the thought. "That's why it's so important to live our lives as happily as possible."

"Happily," Eddy snorted. "Death doesn't care if you're happy or not."

"Don't be so glum," Samantha sighed. "At least we can enjoy the time that we have."

"Maybe," Eddy frowned.

"Why did you say that?" Walt abruptly asked.

"Say what?" Eddy glanced over at him.

"Why did you say, unless you are murdered?" Walt turned his dark brown eyes towards Eddy. "We weren't talking about murder."

"No, we weren't, but it's always a possibility," Eddy explained.

"There must be a reason why you brought it up," Walt said and squinted his eyes at Eddy. He didn't let things go very easily.

Eddy cringed and looked over his shoulder at the gathering again. "All right, but this is just between us, understand?" he shifted his dark blue eyes to Samantha, and then to Walt.

"Between us," Walt agreed.

Samantha nodded and turned her full attention on him. "What is it?" she asked.

"There's some suspicion that James did not die of a heart attack," Eddy said in a low voice. "There's no proof yet, but apparently his skin turned very pink and had a strange rash which doesn't usually occur in this type of death."

"Wow," Walt said with a raised eyebrow. "That is unexpected."

"Even if it wasn't a heart attack, that doesn't mean that it was murder," Samantha said thoughtfully. "It could have been a stroke, or something else."

"It could have been," Eddy agreed and lowered his eyes. "Or it could have been poison."

"Poison?" Samantha gasped.

"Shh!" Eddy said sharply. "Do you want all of Sage Gardens to hear you?"

"Sorry," Samantha grimaced and glanced at

the gathering in the square. "Could you imagine if they did? Everyone would be terrified."

"Panic is never good," Walt said gravely. "Do you really think it was poison, Eddy?" he asked.

"I'm not sure yet," Eddy admitted. "It's going to be up to the medical examiner to decide that."

"I hope it's a good one," Samantha sighed. "I've written about a lot of crimes over the years that were botched by the medical examiner."

"He's a good one," Eddy said with confidence. "I've worked with him many times."

"Oh?" Samantha asked. "I didn't know that you still had connections with the police department."

"Some old timers," Eddy nodded casually. "Sometimes even the young detectives want a little advice if they are stumped on a case."

"How interesting," Samantha said. "We should get together sometime and compare notes about the crimes we've studied."

"Well, I think my point of view would be quite

a bit different from yours," Eddy suggested with a faint smirk. "There's a difference between wielding a gun and wielding a pen."

"I'm aware of that," Samantha said with exasperation. "But sometimes it takes an outside view to see a crime clearly."

"Clearly," Eddy said dismissively, as if putting an end to the conversation.

"About this murder," Walt interjected. "What will the medical examiner have to do to figure out if it was poison or not?"

"First he'll examine the body for natural causes of death. If he finds anything suspicious then he will probably run a tox screen on James' blood. If he was poisoned, it should show up in the tox screen," he frowned. "Well, hopefully."

"Hopefully?" Walt asked.

"There are some poisons that won't show up," Samantha explained. "I wrote about this fascinating crime where a woman killed three of her husbands before they realized she was the one doing it. She was using a poison that wasn't detected by traditional methods."

"I'm sure her husbands didn't find it fascinating," Eddy snapped. Samantha looked over into his glaring eyes.

"Take it easy, Eddy," she said. "I just meant that it was fascinating that she could get away with it for so long."

Eddy shook his head. "That's the problem with you crime journalists, it's all about the drama and the story. But you never see the body, you never see the real consequences of the crime."

"As I said, different perspectives," Samantha said through a tight smile. She was doing her best to remain positive. She decided to attempt to distract both men from the subject. "I think that we should do our own investigation," she suggested.

"It's best left to the police," Walt said sternly.

"I am the police," Eddy reminded him.

"Were the police," Walt corrected him.

"It will take time for the results of the tox screen to come back," Samantha explained. "We should do something in the meantime."

"That's if the medical examiner even orders one," Eddy added.

"I don't know," Walt hesitated. "Is this something we could get in trouble for?"

"Not if we don't get caught," Samantha said with a sly smile.

"We won't get in trouble," Eddy assured Walt. "I don't think it's a bad idea. I'm sure that anything we find could only help the police."

"Then it's decided," Samantha said with a nod. "First thing in the morning we'll meet down by the lake to discuss the case."

"All right," Walt finally agreed. "But I'm not doing anything illegal."

"Don't worry, Walt," Eddy said with a light wink. "We won't let you get your hands dirty."

"Good," Walt said and picked up his watering can again. "But I'm still not going to the vigil."

"Fine, Sam, will you join me?" Eddy asked and offered her his arm.

"You want to go to the vigil?" she asked with surprise as Eddy was not exactly social himself.

"Yes, I do," he replied. "Murderers sometimes like to participate in the aftermath of their crime. If someone did poison James, then there's a good chance that person will be at the vigil."

"You think it was someone here at Sage Gardens?" Samantha asked nervously.

"I think everyone is a suspect, until they're not," Eddy replied with a smirk. "Shall we?"

"Yes," Samantha nodded. Walt glanced over at the two of them.

"Good luck," he muttered, and turned back to his herbs.

# Chapter Five

Eddy was quiet as he walked towards the square with Samantha's arm wrapped around his. He rather enjoyed the warmth of her being close. He was not the romantic type, but there were times when he missed what he had with his wife, just the comfort of companionship. His attention shifted from Samantha to the group of people gathered at the vigil. Samantha pulled her arm from his and focused her attention on the gathering as well.

"It is a sad moment when we lose a friend," Bethany Dander was saying at the front of the group. Bethany took any chance there was to steal the spotlight. She liked to be in front of people. She had once been a fairly well-known actress in plays, but that time had passed quite long ago. Bethany still craved the attention, and others were mostly happy to give it to her.

"Yes, it is," a man's voice called out from the group. Samantha glanced over to see Owen amidst the group. Eddy nodded to him.

"Isn't that nice that he would take time from his own personal life to attend the vigil," Samantha said quietly to Eddy.

"Owen is a good guy," Eddy nodded with a hint of pride in his voice. Samantha hid a fond smile. She could tell that Eddy had a lot more invested in Owen than just a conversation here and there. He seemed to really care about the young nurse. Eddy was scanning the crowd intently. Samantha looked at the people around her curiously. But she had no idea what she was looking for. Though she had researched many crimes over the years for her articles, she had never really seen many criminals face to face. For a moment she wondered if Eddy knew of some special characteristic that they all shared.

"Is he here?" she asked in a whisper. "The murderer?"

Eddy glanced over at her, his rough features growing even rougher with his annoyed expression. "Now, how am I supposed to know?"

he asked gruffly. "Do you think I'm some kind of psychic?"

"I just thought maybe you could tell," Samantha pointed out with a sigh. Eddy sometimes had a way of making her feel just a little bit dense.

"If murderers wore a sign that said 'hey look at me I'm a murderer', no one would ever get killed," Eddy snapped in return then he shook his head. "Well, maybe a few still would, but most wouldn't."

"There's really no need to be mean about it, Eddy," Samantha muttered. Her positive attitude was disintegrating beneath his surly demeanor. He glanced at her once and then back out at the crowd.

"I was not being mean, Sam," he offered. "It's just that I'm trying to focus. The person who did this won't be wearing a sign, but they might be behaving a little differently than the others. Maybe the person will be fidgeting and nervous, or maybe overly grief-stricken. Maybe the person will stand at the edge of the crowd, or maybe the person will take center stage."

"Like Bethany you mean," Samantha suggested and then quickly amended her statement. "I don't mean Bethany is the murderer, I just mean that the person might behave the way she is."

"Possibly," Eddy said with a nod. "Of course, if there even was a murder, the person responsible for it might not even be here. It's just as important to pay attention to who isn't here, as it is to focus on who is."

"I can do that," Samantha said with confidence. She was very skilled at observation so she knew the names and faces of just about all of the residents at Sage Gardens. She would know who was missing. Other than Walt, she noticed that Jo was not present. Also their newest resident, Frank, was not present, which was not too surprising to Samantha considering the way he was handling his grief. Saul was also not there, but he had a difficult time getting around with the gout he was suffering. Annabelle who was usually one of the most social women that Samantha knew was also notably absent. It was strange how suddenly people she would never even consider the least bit violent, were becoming her main suspects in a murder.

As the vigil began to break up, Eddy nodded at her. "I think we got what we came for."

"We did?" she asked. "Do you know who it is?"

"I don't yet," he explained. "But when I have my suspects or think I know who they might be, I'll be able to remember how they acted tonight. Do you want me to walk you to your villa?" he offered.

Samantha regarded him with some confusion.

"Eddy, I can't ever figure you out," she said.

"What do you mean?" he asked with a furrowed brow.

"One minute you're cruel and insulting, the next you're acting like a gentleman," she shook her head.

"You know what I'll never figure out, Sam?" he asked and settled his arms across his stomach.

"What?" she asked.

"Why a woman can't simply say yes or no, to a question," he said and then spun on his heel. Samantha watched as he stalked off towards his villa. She was as confused as ever.

Eddy shoved his hands deep into his pockets and grumbled under his breath as he walked back towards his villa. He knew that he had been a little rough with Samantha, but it irritated him that he couldn't simply offer to walk someone home without there being an issue.

"Cruel am I?" he asked the shadows around him. "I've never been cruel."

"I doubt that is true, detective," a voice drifted from the darkness beside him. It was rather sultry, and definitely feminine. It drew his attention right away. He spun into a defensive stance towards the voice.

"Who's there?" he asked sharply.

"Relax," the voice said evenly. "I'm not anyone to worry yourself about," she stepped out of the darkness. Jo swept her black hair back over her shoulder and peered at Eddy curiously. "I just happened to be walking past."

"Oh, did you?" he asked as he surveyed her intently. "And eavesdropping?"

"Can you call it eavesdropping if you're talking to yourself?" Jo questioned with a light laugh. "Or maybe you're concerned that I'm going to get that handsome nurse to up your meds."

Eddy glowered at her impatiently. "I'm not on any meds."

"Oh," Jo said in a long, drawn out breath. "Well, I guess that explains a lot."

"Just who are you?" Eddy demanded as he studied her. He had seen her around but never met her.

"My name is Jo," she replied though there was some hesitation in her voice. "Like I said, I was just passing by."

"All right, well keep on going," Eddy gestured to the walkway ahead of him.

"Aren't you even going to tell me your name?" Jo asked. Her gaze was damning between thick, dark lashes.

"It's Eddy," he replied begrudgingly.

"Nice to meet you, Eddy," Jo said before she walked past him and across the grass. He turned to watch her walk away, and didn't regret it. The way she walked made it clear that she hadn't lost any of her confidence over the years. Eddy couldn't deny that she was beautiful, but that didn't mean much to him. He'd put handcuffs on plenty of beautiful women. With a shake of his head he turned and continued walking down the walkway towards his villa. He had a lot on his mind. There was no room for Jo in his thoughts.

# Chapter Six

The sun rose over Sage Gardens the next morning, but the usual cheerful atmosphere was missing. There were no joggers making their way around the lake. No one was walking a little dog yipping with urgency to empty its bladder. Walt noticed the change in the surroundings right away. He sipped his coffee and looked out of his front window at the strangely desolate setting. It left him unsettled when things were different. He drank out of the same mug each morning. He bought the same brand of coffee. He added exactly the same amount of milk. Things made sense when they were the same. Otherwise, there would be chaos. Even though the morning was quiet, but for the birds tweeting in the trees, Walt felt as if he was immersed in chaos.

"Where is everyone?" he finally wondered out loud. Then he remembered. James was dead. Most people were probably hiding out in their villas, not wanting to be the first person to emerge and act as if things were back to normal. It would be offensive to do that of course. It wasn't like there hadn't been a few deaths at Sage Gardens. But for some reason the fact that James, a seemingly fit and healthy man, had died on his birthday made this death hit the residents a little harder.

Walt then remembered that he was supposed to be meeting Eddy and Samantha down by the lake to discuss the investigation into whether James had been murdered. Walt still felt uneasy about getting involved. His career as an accountant had caused him to encounter many different types of people. His mindset was always to stay out of their personal business and focus only on numbers. Numbers didn't kill people.

He finished the last of his coffee and washed the mug. He set the mug in its place on the shelf above the sink. Then he walked over to the door and slipped his shoes on. He tied them carefully. He stood up and opened the door to the villa. He drew a long breath before stepping out into the world. He much preferred to hide away and only interact on his own terms. As he was walking down towards the lake he saw Samantha walking towards it as well. He raised his hand to wave to her, but she looked fairly distracted. Walt looked past her up towards the main square and the recreation hall. He noticed that Owen and Eddy were talking. He sighed as he realized there was no turning back now, he was ankle deep in what might turn out to be a murder investigation.

***

Eddy intended to be the first down by the lake. He had been awake most of the night, partially because of his encounter with Jo and the strange familiarity he felt with her, but also because he was thinking about James. The more he considered the possibility that he had been poisoned, the more sense it made to him. James was far too healthy to drop dead of a heart attack. But he had died in a hall full of witnesses. When

65

he walked down towards the lake he took the long way past the recreation hall. He wanted to see if anyone was hanging around. He looked up at the sound of someone calling his name.

"Eddy," Owen called out and waved to him as he jogged across the courtyard in front of the main office.

"Owen," Eddy nodded and adjusted his hat. "Is everything all right?"

"Yes, I guess," Owen replied. He glanced around to be sure that no one else was in ear shot. Then he looked back at Eddy. "The medical examiner called me. He wanted to know the details of James' death and he asked me to put any remaining food and drink aside from the party as they were going to come and bag it for analysis."

"Oh really?" Eddy asked, quite intrigued. He didn't want to jump the gun. "Did he say why?"

"He said he had some suspicions, but wouldn't know anything solid until the tox screen comes in. I just thought that you would want to know," he added and couldn't hide a slight smile.

"We were right."

"In this case I think it would be better if we were wrong," Eddy sighed and shook his head. He caught sight of Samantha and Walt talking near the lake.

"Who do you think would have done it?" Owen asked quickly. "If he was poisoned I mean. Do you think it was someone at the party?"

"Don't start lining up suspects, Owen," Eddy warned him. "As far as we know, it's still natural causes. If you start looking at people funny, the killer, if there is one, might get tipped off."

"Oh, good point," Owen nodded and then smiled at Eddy. "I am learning so much from you."

"Well, I don't know how much of it will help you in doctor school," Eddy pointed out.

"You'd be surprised," Owen said. "Often finding the cause of an illness is a lot like being a detective."

"Well, then I'm sure that you'll be a great

one," Eddy said and offered one of his rare genuine smiles.

"Thanks, Eddy," Owen smiled in return.

"Can anyone help me?" a voice called out from just in front of the main office. Owen glanced over his shoulder. It was Mike, James' son.

"Excuse me, I have to help Mike collect his father's things," Owen explained and walked away from Eddy quickly. Eddy narrowed his eyes as he watched Owen walk towards Mike. He didn't exactly seem heartbroken over the loss of his father, but then, grief didn't always show on the surface. Sometimes it hid deep below. Still, Eddy thought it might not be a bad idea to observe a little longer.

"I just went to my father's villa to collect his things," Mike said sharply. "I found all of his stuff boxed up."

"Yes, some of the staff got together and did that. We always do that for deceased residents. We thought it would be easier for you that way," Owen explained with a half-hearted smile. "Is it a problem?"

"It's a problem when things are stolen from his villa," Mike barked in return. Eddy felt the urge to intervene. He didn't like to see Owen spoken to that way. But he restrained himself. He knew that Owen could handle himself.

"Stolen? What was stolen?" Owen asked with disbelief.

"My father's watch. Actually, it was his father's watch. It is very valuable and it is nowhere to be found," Mike growled.

"Perhaps he was wearing it?" Owen suggested. "Maybe he wanted to wear it since it was a special occasion?"

"If that were the case then the medical examiner would have it," Mike said through gritted teeth. "I've already called him. He does not have any watch."

"Wow," Owen lowered his eyes for a moment as if considering what to say. "Let me go to his villa with you. Maybe it's just been overlooked."

"No, it was not overlooked," Mike snapped. "I looked through the whole villa and all of the boxes. What kind of place is this?" Mike demanded as he stepped closer to Owen. "I trusted you to take care of my father. I was told by the owners of this place that it was safe, now he's dead, and his watch has been stolen. Is that what happens here? One of the residents dies so everything they have in their villa is fair game?"

"Sir, I'm sorry for you loss," Owen said sympathetically. "I know that this is a difficult time. I can certainly convey your concerns to the owners, and also offer you their contact information. However, you should know that I am the nurse here. I am not in charge of the villas, or the security of residents' possessions."

"Whatever," Mike shook his head, clearly aggravated. "All I want is my father's watch. I want all of the employees searched. You know what, I want all of the residents searched as well."

Owen sighed and reached into his pocket. He pulled out his wallet and sorted through it until he found the business card that he was looking for. He held it out to Mike.

"You'll have to call the owners if you want that done," he explained.

"Or maybe I'll just call the police," Mike snapped back. He took the business card and tucked it safely into his pocket.

"Again, I am very sorry for your loss," Owen said with genuine sympathy. "If I find out any information about your father's watch I will let you know."

"You do just that," Mike growled. "If anyone has any decency in this place, that watch will turn up."

"Like I said, if I hear anything, I'll call," Owen replied in a sterner voice. He met Mike's eyes with an unwavering stare.

"Will you at least help me load up the boxes?" Mike relented.

"Gladly," Owen replied. The two men began to walk off towards James' villa. Eddy watched them go, then he turned and began walking down towards the lake. Mike's outrage was warranted, but something about the way he was being so demanding made Eddy wonder if all he truly cared about were his father's valuables.

When he reached the bench and canopy where Samantha and Walt were sitting, he was still lost in thought.

"What was that about?" Walt asked.

"Huh?" Eddy glanced up at him.

"What were you and Owen talking about?" Walt asked more specifically.

"Owen informed me that the medical examiner has run a tox screen and is waiting for the results. The medical examiner asked for the remaining food and drink from the party, so I think he thinks it might have been poisoned," he frowned and glanced back towards James' old villa. "Apparently, when James' son arrived to collect his things, his father's antique watch was missing. He's insisting that someone from Sage Gardens stole it."

"How terrible," Samantha said and shook her head with disgust. "I remember him wearing that watch on occasion. It was certainly eye-catching."

"Someone stole the poor man's watch," Walt said gravely. He lightly touched the watch on his own wrist, as if to make sure that it was still there. "He's not even in the grave. Who would be so cruel?"

"Was that all that was taken?" Samantha asked. She was intrigued by the missing watch, as it was possible that the same person who killed James also stole his watch.

"So far it seems to be," Eddy replied. "If anything else is missing then I am sure that Mike will let everyone know. He's already on the warpath about it."

Walt shook his head and glared down at his shoes. "I can take a lot of things, Eddy, but I can't tolerate a thief."

"Maybe the watch was just misplaced," Eddy suggested with a mild shrug. "In the chaos of a sudden death, sometimes things go missing, only to be found in a strange place later."

"Seems suspicious though, doesn't it?" Samantha asked. "First a murder and now a theft."

"We don't know that either are what they seem just yet," Eddy reminded them.

"Hey, remember that Mike brought his father his very own cupcake," Samantha said out of the blue. "If the medical examiner requested leftover food and drink to be examined he must suspect that the poison was in the food. It couldn't have been in the cake, because we all ate that."

"But James was the only one to eat the gluten-free cupcake," Walt agreed.

"You know, Mike had just come back into James' life," Eddy pointed out gravely. "I'm not sure what their falling out was about, but I know it kept them from talking for years."

"Yes, there was some big argument between them when James was younger," Walt nodded as he recalled a conversation that he had with James.

"I thought it was great that the two of them began talking again. At least, on his final day, James was with his son."

"Which is rather coincidental, don't you think?" Eddy pressed and tried to meet Walt's eyes. Walt was busy fidgeting with the cuff of his sleeve which was slightly shorter than the other.

"What are you implying, Eddy?" he asked and glanced up abruptly to meet Eddy's eyes.

"I'm just pointing out that it seems awfully convenient that James' son makes up with him, then suddenly he dies of a supposed heart attack, with Mike right by his side," Eddy shrugged. "Call me cynical but sometimes bad blood doesn't heal, sometimes it just gets worse."

"That is cynical," Samantha said with a slight shake of her head. "But it's not necessarily wrong. I think we need to consider Mike as a suspect. He had the opportunity with that sole cupcake he made."

"He looked pretty happy to be with his father though," Walt pointed out.

"Happiness is easily faked," Eddy said.

Samantha glanced over at him, but she didn't argue with him, instead she took a deep breath.

"Okay, well I think we need to find out who stole the watch. Maybe that will give us a bit more information about what really happened. Eddy, why don't you talk to some of the staff and see if you can find out who might have been in or near James' room yesterday?"

"I can do that," he agreed.

"I'll see what I can get from the party committee," Samantha offered.

"You mean the gossip committee," Eddy laughed a little.

"They always know everything that is going on, so it won't hurt to ask," Samantha pointed out.

"I can dig into Mike's financials," Walt said with a slow smile. "I still know how to get just about all of the information that I would need. If you want to know why someone would be murdered, the first place you should look is the money."

"That would be great," Samantha said with a proud smile. "I knew that there was a way to figure all of this out."

"All of this is going to mean nothing if the tox screen comes back clear," Eddy pointed out grimly.

"Well, if it comes back clear then we will have just had a little adventure looking into things. If it doesn't, then we will have information to help the police get justice for James," Samantha argued in return. She could tell that Eddy was feeling uncertain about the investigation. "What could be wrong with that?"

"What could be wrong with that is that we are invading the life and privacy of a man who just lost his father," Eddy pointed out. "I don't think we should stop, but I do think that we need to be delicate about it."

"Delicate," Walt nodded. "Don't worry, he'll never even know that I was looking into him. As far as I'm concerned money always tells the truth.

If you find the money trail, you will find the reality of a situation. But I understand what you're saying about his grief. It might set him off if he knew that we were considering him a suspect. It's a horrible thing to think that a son could kill his own father."

"It's been done before," Eddy said quietly. The things he had seen in his time as a detective were written across his face in the form of a haunted expression. "Far too many times."

"Well, since we don't have any other leads, I think that Mike is as good as any place to start," Samantha said. "So, Walt look into Mike's finances, and James' if you can. Eddy, maybe you could ask the staff if they had seen any arguments between Mike and James."

"Aren't you just skilled at delegation?" he asked as he smiled at Samantha.

"I'm just trying to keep things organized," Samantha replied defensively.

"I wasn't complaining," Eddy adjusted his hat. Then he turned and walked off towards the recreation hall.

"You okay?" Walt asked Samantha who was staring off after Eddy.

"I think so," Samantha frowned. "I'll be better when we find out who did this to James."

# Chapter Seven

Samantha returned to her villa to change. She had to be dressed a certain way to have a conversation with anyone on the party committee. As she was sorting through the choices hanging in her closet, her mind drifted back over the last time she had chosen so carefully what she would wear. It was for her retirement party from the last magazine she had worked for. It was a special night, and though she was looking forward to her retirement, it had been bittersweet as well. Sometimes she missed the bustle of the magazine office. She always had one or two friends at work that she could bounce her ideas or articles off to get their opinion. She found it difficult now to make friends at Sage Gardens. Since Baki had left Eddy and Walt were the closest friends she had, and that was fairly sad considering that they barely ever spent time together.

She chose a blouse and skirt and changed into

them. As she was putting away her laundry, she came across a pile of folders in the bottom of her closet. She had kept the information from a few of the cases she had written articles about. Some of them she kept because they were yet unsolved, others she kept because they had such an impact on her. When she saw which folder was on top her heart lurched. All at once she knew exactly why Jo seemed so familiar to her. Samantha didn't believe it at first. She snatched up the folder and walked over to her bed. She sat down on the edge of it and flipped the folder open. Inside were several handwritten pages of her own notes, as well as the printed research that she had done on the case.

It was the case of an infamous cat burglar who managed to steal from some of the wealthiest and most well-known names before she was caught. Samantha had followed her for years before she turned herself in. That was the part that had stuck in Samantha's mind to make the case unique. Joanne could have gotten away with everything, the police had no clue who she was, but she voluntarily turned herself in and confessed to the crimes.

On one of the printed pages was a photograph of Joanne on the day she turned herself in. Samantha stared down at her voluminous, black hair, her haunted, dark eyes, and the sneer on her lips. She was sure that the Joanne in the picture was the same woman that she knew as Jo at Sage Gardens. But that had to be impossible. Joanne should have still been in prison. With a trembling hand Samantha dialed the phone number of a contact she still had in the prison system. She asked about Joanne's current status.

"She was released about three months ago," he explained. "She qualified for early release because of good behavior."

"Any idea where she is now?" Samantha asked nervously.

"Sorry, that information I can't access," he replied. "Is everything okay?"

"Oh sure," Samantha forced a smile into her voice. "I was just doing a follow up article on her and the crimes she committed."

"I thought you were retired?" he asked.

"Does a writer ever really retire?" she countered with a short laugh.

"I guess not," he replied. Samantha exchanged a few more pleasantries with him before hanging up the phone. She stared down at the picture in complete shock. She was sure that she must be imagining things. Just because Joanne had been released, that didn't mean that she would be at Sage Gardens. What were the chances of that happening? She put the folders away in the closet, determined to put the idea out of her mind. But the moment she stepped out of her villa she caught sight of Jo walking towards the mailboxes in the main square. Samantha couldn't resist. She had to know for sure.

Samantha did her best to match her footsteps to Jo's as she approached the mailboxes. She didn't want to alert the woman to the fact that she was being followed. Samantha had to be sure that she was right. Jo walked up to the mailboxes. She reached into the pocket of her tight jeans and pulled out a small key. She pushed the key into one of the metal boxes and turned it. Samantha watched Jo pull out a few envelopes. Then she locked the box again. She pushed the key into her pocket. She took a deep breath. An instant later she was directly in front of Samantha as if she had been there the entire time.

"Why are you following me?" she asked through gritted teeth. She glared into Samantha's eyes. Samantha's breath caught in her throat. She had written many things about crime in the past, articles in particular about Jo, but she had never been face to face with a proven criminal.

"I wasn't," Samantha said quickly. "I was just going to get my mail."

"Oh?" Jo asked and then raised an eyebrow. "Where is your key?"

"Huh?" Samantha mumbled.

"Your key, if you're going to get the mail, then

84

you should have your key," Jo insisted and took a slight step back. "So, show me your key."

Samantha's mouth felt dry. She wasn't sure if she could even speak. She was looking into the eyes of a woman she had written articles about for several years when she was younger. This wasn't just another person who was encroaching on her personal space, Joanne was a legend.

"I must have forgotten it," Samantha managed to stumble out. "I thought I had it, and now I don't."

"Sure," Jo nodded and folded her arms across her stomach. "Why were you following me?" she demanded.

"I just thought you looked familiar," Samantha admitted. "You look like someone I used to know."

"I highly doubt that you ever knew me," Jo countered and glowered at her. "So, how could I be familiar to you?"

Samantha knew that she was running out of

excuses. She hadn't planned on actually confronting Jo. She was just going to follow her and see if she could confirm if she was who she thought she was. Suddenly, Samantha thought about the stolen watch. Could Jo have been the one to steal it? Would a cat burglar stoop so low?

"My mistake," Samantha said nervously and started to back away from her. "I'm sorry to have bothered you really, I won't bother you again."

Jo continued to stare directly at her. Her eyes narrowed even tighter, so that they were tiny slits of judgment.

"So, you're not going to be writing anything about me?" she asked.

Samantha suddenly felt ice-cold. She knew that she was staring with wide eyes at Jo for far too long. Jo obviously knew exactly who Samantha was and she had no idea how to respond to that question.

"I'm retired," she finally said, her voice wavering.

"So am I," Jo replied sternly. "So, why don't we both just continue with our retirement? Sound good?"

"I think so," Samantha replied hesitantly.

"Listen, I don't know why you're following me around. I don't really care to. But please make sure you don't snoop around me again," she said with ice-cold eyes. "Understand?"

Samantha started to nod in agreement and with gratitude, then something inside of her shifted. This was Joanne, she had no doubt. This was the very cat burglar that she had written so many scathing pieces about. This was the woman who might have gone into a dead man's villa and taken his very valuable watch. Why should she back down from her? Samantha could call the FBI and have them on Jo's back immediately. If she was found guilty, as a repeat offender, she might never be free again.

"Are you threatening me?" Samantha heard herself ask with more bravery than she expected to wield.

"Should I be?" Jo asked and quirked a brow. "Why don't you just tell me what you're getting at?" Jo demanded as she let her hands fall back to her sides. "If we're not pretending that we don't have a clue who each other is anymore, then just be straight with me. I know that you have been watching me for a while. So, why are you after me now? There's no bounty on my head. I did my time."

"James' very expensive watch is missing," Samantha blurted out before she could stop herself. "The man who died yesterday."

"And?" Jo asked with confusion. "What does a dead man's watch have to do with me?"

"Uh well," Samantha cleared her throat and glanced around nervously before looking back at Jo. "It's a very valuable watch."

"You can't be serious," Jo shook her head with disbelief. "Are you really accusing me of petty theft? From a corpse?"

"Don't talk about James that way," Samantha snapped back sharply. "He was a good man."

"I'm sure you knew him well," Jo said smugly.

"What do you mean by that?" Samantha asked defensively.

"Well let's see, you're following me around because you think I stole his watch, so I assumed that you two must have had more than a casual relationship," Jo explained slowly as if Samantha would have a difficult time comprehending what she was saying.

"We were just acquaintances," Samantha corrected and then pursed her lips. "I just hate to see any kind of crime invade the safety of Sage Gardens."

"Oh please, I know that you're not that naïve," Jo shook her head. "Listen, I didn't swipe the dead man's watch. I don't really care who did. I would appreciate not being stalked when I'm picking up my mail."

With that she turned on her heel and walked away from Samantha with sharp swings of her hips. Samantha shook her head and finally drew a full breath. She wasn't quite sure what to think about their encounter. Perhaps the most shocking revelation was that Jo knew exactly who she was.

Samantha felt confident that Jo was telling her the truth. Now that she could think about it calmly she didn't really think that a retired thief of her caliber would stoop so low as to steal a watch. Joanne had been responsible for one of the most infamous art heists. Just when she expected Joanne to disappear around the corner, the woman suddenly stopped. She took a deep breath and then turned around. She walked back towards Samantha. Samantha felt nervous as she watched the woman approach her. She considered running but the opportunity to do so quickly passed as Joanne crossed the distance. She was still frozen in place when Joanne stopped in front of her.

"Look, the truth is, I'm trying to start a new life," Jo explained. "The last thing I want to do is get involved in all of this, but if you want my help finding out who stole the watch, I can do that in order to prove that it wasn't me."

"How?" Samantha asked and avoided looking

directly at her.

"I still have some connections," Jo explained. "If someone stole that watch, I know exactly who they would sell it to."

"And you would be willing to tell me?" Samantha asked with genuine surprise. Jo stared at her for a long moment.

"Don't think that just because you wrote all of those articles about me, you know anything about me," Jo replied sternly. "I am willing to help you, in exchange for you keeping my secret. I really don't want to become the resident felon."

"Even if you are?" Samantha asked before thinking about whether it was a good idea.

Jo pursed her lips impatiently. "The past is in the past, Samantha. So, do we have a deal?" she asked and extended her hand towards her. Samantha's heartbeat quickened. She could not believe that she was about to shake the hand of such a notorious woman. She took Jo's hand in a firm handshake, but she couldn't quite meet her eyes.

"We have a deal," she said.

"I'll contact you when I have a name," Jo replied. Then she walked off casually. Samantha's heart was still racing with the impact of the encounter. She forgot all about talking to the party committee until Carolyn Taylor walked up behind her with a laugh.

"Well, aren't you dressed up, Samantha," she said, though Samantha wasn't sure if it was an insult or a compliment.

"Carolyn, I was hoping to run into you," Samantha said and swallowed thickly. She tried to force her mind away from Jo.

"Well, you have," Carolyn said cheerfully, then her smile faded. "If this is about joining I just don't think that you're the right fit."

Samantha willed herself not to glare at the woman. "No, it's not about joining. I was wondering if you or any of your friends noticed anything unusual while you were setting up for the party."

"I'm not sure what you mean," Carolyn admitted.

"I mean, did you notice anyone acting strangely. Maybe someone came in early that didn't need to be there? Someone that wasn't part of organizing the party?" Samantha suggested as she studied her intently.

"No, no one," Carolyn said thoughtfully. "Well, we did invite Frank over to help us with the set up," she explained.

"Frank? Why?" Samantha asked with shock. "He just moved in, and you let him join?"

"He's single," Carolyn replied dismissively. Samantha couldn't hide her surprise.

"So, Frank was there with you while you were setting up?"

"Well, no," she said. "He seemed eager to help at first and then after a few minutes he said he forgot he had something to do and he just left."

"Was there anyone else?" Samantha asked.

"No, that was it," Carolyn shook her head.

"Mike dropped off the food shortly after."

"Mike dropped off the food?" Samantha repeated.

"Yes," Carolyn replied. "He organized the catering for the party which was really nice of him. We usually have to organize it but because of his father's specific dietary needs he offered to do it so that there was enough choice for Frank to eat."

"Anything else you can remember," Samantha asked thoughtfully.

"No, that's it," Carolyn shook her head.

"Thanks for your time, Carolyn," Samantha said as she reached into her purse for her notebook.

"Sure," Carolyn replied brightly. "Samantha, can I be honest with you?" she asked.

"Okay," Samantha said and looked up at her warily.

"Most of the ladies in the group would be fine with you joining. The problem is that one in particular has her eye on John 'Eddy' Edwards, and he won't even look in her direction," she explained with a smug smile. "Don't tell anyone that I told you that though."

"She likes Eddy?" Samantha asked and offered a mild shrug. "What does that have to do with me?"

"She thinks the two of you have something going on," Carolyn explained. Samantha stared at her with disbelief. She couldn't fathom the idea that she had been blacklisted because she associated with someone that one of the women in the group had an interest in.

"This isn't high school," she blurted out. "That is complete nonsense."

"I'm just telling you what I know," Carolyn smiled. "As a friend."

"Wow, well there's nothing going on between us," Samantha said and lifted her hands in the air. "Trust me, if she wants him he's all hers. Although, I have a hard time thinking of Eddy in a relationship."

"You must be blind," Carolyn said with surprise. "He's so handsome, and he once wore a badge."

"Okay," Samantha said slowly. "Anyway, if you hear anything about James, anything suspicious, please let me know."

"I will," Carolyn smiled again. Then she hurried off towards the recreation hall. Samantha was left to digest the information she had just been given. Was Eddy as handsome as Carolyn claimed? Samantha had never really noticed.

# Chapter Eight

Eddy pushed open the heavy door to the recreation hall. It was quiet inside with all of the chairs and tables folded up and stowed away. The recreation hall was used for many things from parties, to bingo tournaments, as well as silent auctions.

Eddy thought it would be the best place to start for questioning the staff since some might have been working the day of the party. The community hired janitors as well as security guards to keep everything in order at Sage Gardens. Basically, the staff took care of all of the little things that most residents didn't want to be bothered with.

"Hello?" Eddy called out as he walked further into the recreation hall. He could smell the strong scent of a floor cleaner so he knew that someone had recently been cleaning.

"Working," a muffled voice called back from

the bathrooms. Eddy walked towards the bathroom. He had just about reached it when the door swung open. Dale, one of the janitors on staff, glared at him.

"Seriously? I just cleaned that floor," he said with frustration. Eddy glanced down at his shoes. They weren't very dirty, but they had still left small marks on the clean floor.

"Sorry about that," he said with genuine remorse.

"No one is supposed to be in here while I'm cleaning," Dale said impatiently. He was a young man, in his early twenties. He carried a chip on his shoulder that reminded Eddy of the delinquents he used to deal with on a regular basis.

"Take it easy, Dale," Eddy said. "I just wanted to ask you a few questions."

"I'm a little busy," Dale pointed out as he picked up the mop that had been resting against the wall beside the bathroom door.

"It's about James," Eddy explained.

"Oh," Dale lowered his eyes. He gripped the broom handle tightly. "That was a sad thing."

"Yes, it was," Eddy agreed and noted the way that Dale was hanging onto the broom handle. "I just thought you might have noticed if he'd been out of sorts. Or maybe if someone asked about him."

"I don't exactly keep track of those kinds of things," Dale said and looked up at Eddy. "What does it matter anyway? He had a heart attack."

"Oh, I know he did," Eddy nodded. He didn't want to alarm Dale with the notion that it could have been murder. "However, someone went into his room after he passed and stole his watch. A watch that his son was meant to inherit."

"So?" Dale asked grimly.

"I thought you might have noticed if someone had been in his room. Or maybe you would know who cleaned it?" Eddy suggested and took a step closer to the janitor.

"I cleaned it," Dale said and narrowed his eyes

as he looked at Eddy. "I've got nothing to say about the watch."

"Did you notice anyone going in or out of his room after his passing?" Eddy asked as he stepped even closer, essentially pinning Dale between himself and the wall.

"I didn't see anything," Dale insisted, but his eyes flicked away from Eddy when he spoke. Eddy knew exactly what that meant. When someone wanted him to believe something because they meant it, they would look him right in the eyes. But when someone wanted him to believe something that was a lie, they would do everything but.

"Who was it?" Eddy pressed, ignoring the denial. "Did you see the person, did they pay you off? Is that it?" he asked, his voice escalating slowly but hardening with intensity as well.

"Look, old man, I don't know what you're talking about," Dale growled and tried to move past Eddy. Eddy shifted in the same direction. It prevented Dale from getting past him, without ever touching him. It was another trick he had learned in his days of wearing a badge.

"Not so fast, Dale," he said sharply. "I'm asking you a simple question. I expect an answer. I know you know something, you might as well tell me now, because I will find out."

"Why should I tell you anything?" Dale snapped. His forehead was dotted with shiny drops of sweat. His face had gotten a little pale as they spoke. "It's not like you're the police or anything. I don't have to talk to you. Besides, I saw the way that guy, Mike, talked to his dad. He didn't deserve that watch."

"What do you mean you saw the way Mike talked to James?"

"A couple of weeks ago," Dale replied. "I was cleaning the villa next to James' and I heard arguing. So, I ducked my head out to see what was going on. James and Mike were standing there shouting at each other about money. Mike was talking about how much money James had, and James was saying that it was none of Mike's business."

"Sounds pretty vicious," Eddy said. "Did they say anything else?"

"I don't know," Dale shrugged. "Unlike you, if it isn't my business, I stay out of it. I just went back to cleaning. But if you ask me, he didn't deserve to inherit a dime, so I don't really care about a missing watch."

"But you do know who stole it?" Eddy posed the question again with increased determination.

"No," Dale argued and again tried to get past Eddy. Eddy shifted in the same direction, blocking his escape.

"So, you have something to lose in all of this, Dale?" Eddy demanded. "You're either protecting yourself, or you're protecting someone else."

"I don't know what you're talking about," Dale insisted, though his voice had grown more desperate. "All I do is clean up around here, you know that."

"I think you're hiding something," Eddy

challenged and towered over the young man.

"I'm not," Dale shot back with anger in his voice.

Eddy glared at him, but he took a step back slightly.

"I'll find out if you have anything to do with this," he warned Dale through gritted teeth. "This isn't over."

"Yes, it is," Dale snapped back in return. "Now, if you don't mind, I have work to do!"

Eddy had to clench his jaw to keep from saying something he might regret to Dale. Dale shoved up the sleeves of his shirt and began pushing the mop across the floor once more. Eddy sneered a little as he noticed the snake tattoo that wrapped around the man's forearm.

"Appropriate," he muttered under his breath before he turned and walked out of the hall. As Eddy was storming down the path towards his own villa, he noticed that Samantha was near the mailboxes, talking to one of the women from the party committee. He frowned as he knew he hadn't gotten much information. He hoped that Walt and Samantha would have better luck.

***

Walt sat back in his chair and stared at his computer screen. He was more than a little surprised by what he had found. He picked up his phone and dialed Eddy's number.

"Hello?" Eddy asked.

"Can you and Samantha meet me at my place?" Walt asked and tapped a few keys on the keyboard.

"Sure," Eddy replied. "Did you find something?"

"I think it's better to talk about it in person," Walt explained.

"All right, I'll get a hold of Samantha and we'll be over in a few minutes," he said before hanging up the phone. Walt hung up his phone and began paging down through the document in front of him. By the time there was a knock on the door he was lost in the numbers he was calculating. It took a second set of knocks to get him to react.

"Come in," he called out. "It's open!"

The door to his villa swung open. Eddy and Samantha walked in. Samantha walked over to the desk where Walt was seated. Eddy walked up to him on the other side.

"I have some information about James' finances," Walt said and swiveled in his computer chair to face them. He lifted his glasses from his nose and wiped the tender area just beneath each eye. "Computers," he said with a short laugh.

"What did you find?" Samantha asked.

"It turns out James was loaded," Walt said with a shake of his head. "Which makes me wonder how he ended up here. But that doesn't matter now I guess. What matters is that he had plenty of money. Which in my opinion gives people motive to kill."

"Love or money," Eddy nodded in agreement.

"The question is who stood to gain the most from James' death," Samantha said.

"Well, it would be safe to assume that James would leave his fortune to his son. Don't you think?" Eddy asked.

"It's possible, but not definite. Remember they were just recently reunited," Samantha said.

"And it's easy to reconnect when you know that your estranged loved one has plenty of cash to leave behind," Eddy said. His brow creased with disgust.

"Just because Mike reconnected with his father doesn't mean that he was after the money. I know the lawyer that James was meeting with," Samantha said. "I think if we pay him a visit we might be able to find out some more information about his will."

"Lawyers aren't supposed to disclose that kind of information," Eddy narrowed his eyes.

"He's a good friend," Samantha smiled. "I

might be able to get something out of him. Do you want to come with me?"

"Yes," Eddy nodded and snatched up his suit jacket. "Let's see if we can meet him now."

"I'll just give him a call."

Samantha walked into the kitchen to call Nicholas. She had noticed him visiting James' villa only the week before.

"Hello Samantha," Nicholas answered.

"Hi Nicholas. How are you?"

"Glad you called. It's been so long. Are you finally going to take me up on that lunch date?"

"Possibly," she replied. "But I was hoping to get an appointment with you. I have something I'd like to discuss."

"Sure no problem. I don't have anything scheduled for the morning so you could come in at any time."

"Thanks. I'll see you soon," she hung up the phone and walked back into the living room where Eddy was waiting.

"So?" he asked.

"We can go see him now," Samantha picked up her purse and headed for the door. "Let us know if you find out anything interesting, Walt."

"I will," Walt muttered. He was already engrossed in his computer screen again.

Eddy followed after Samantha as she stepped out the door. "I'll drive," he said.

"I don't think so," Samantha laughed and shook her head. "I'm driving."

"Fine."

The drive to Nicholas' office was a fairly long one which was why he mostly met with his Sage Gardens clients at their villas. Thanks to Samantha's recommendation he had quite a few clients in Sage Gardens.

"So, how do you know this guy?" Eddy asked.

"He's an old friend. We worked together on a few things."

"That's an evasive answer."

"Am I under oath?" She laughed and glanced over at him. "You have to work on your social skills."

"All I'm saying is that if someone is evasive with an answer there's usually a reason."

Samantha sighed and rolled her eyes. "Okay. We dated briefly about fifteen years ago. Then he got married. Now he's divorced."

"And he's wondering if he missed a golden opportunity?"

"I think he's just hoping for some company. You know, normal human interaction," she glanced over at him with a slight smile.

"Humans are too complicated," Eddy said as he gazed out the passenger window.

The two fell into silence for the last part of the drive. Samantha parked in front of Nicholas' office. As they walked up to the door together she glanced at Eddy. "Be nice. Remember he's not a suspect."

"Well, we don't know that for sure. He was

James' lawyer and recently visited with him."

"I do know that for sure, Eddy. Nicholas is a friend of mine and he would never hurt anyone," Samantha shot him a look of warning and then opened the door. The office was small with only two chairs in the waiting area. The receptionist's desk was empty.

"Nicholas?" Samantha called out.

"Come on back!" A voice called out from the end of the small hallway. Samantha led the way to the office. Inside a thin man sat behind a small wooden desk.

"Samantha!" He stood up from his chair to greet her. His gaze passed curiously over Eddy. "You brought a friend?"

"A detective," Eddy interjected.

"A retired detective," Samantha said.

"Ah I see. This is a business visit," Nicholas sat back down behind the desk.

"Honestly, it's not quite business either. I was hoping for a favor," Samantha said. She sat down across from him. "It's about James."

"What about him?" Nicholas asked with a perplexed look.

"I'm here because we're beginning to think that James' death was not of natural causes."

"What do you mean?" Nicholas asked.

"It's possible that he was poisoned," Samantha did her best not to look in Eddy's direction. She knew that he would not approve of her sharing so much information.

"What?" Nicholas stood half way up out of his chair and then sank back down. "That makes sense I guess."

Eddy's eyes widened. It was not the reaction he had expected.

"It makes sense?" Samantha asked.

"I just couldn't believe that he died that way. The last time I saw James he was encouraging me to start a jogging regiment. He was a strong and healthy man. For him to just pass so suddenly and so soon after the change to his will seemed odd to me."

"Change to his will?" Samantha pressed.

"Oh uh, you know that information is privileged, Samantha."

"It's okay, Nicholas. It will stay just between us. We're just trying to help."

Nicholas glanced warily at Eddy and then looked back at Samantha. "Look, after James made his fortune I encouraged him to create a will just in case. He was estranged from his son. So, we set up his will so his inheritance would go to his best friend and business partner. They've lost touch over the years, but James didn't want to change it. Then all of a sudden last week he wants everything switched around."

"Let me guess, he wanted to leave it to his son?" Eddy asked.

"Well, I'm not technically allowed to say but I won't say that you're wrong. Listen, James was a good guy. He felt terrible about the bad blood between himself and his son, so I was happy that he had made up with his son, but it all seemed so sudden. Then when he wanted to leave everything to him, I just felt uneasy. I tried to talk him out of it, I suggested a trust, but he didn't want anything to do with it."

"So, Mike stood to inherit all of the money?" Eddy asked.

"He did."

"Then maybe he decided to speed up the timeline of his inheritance," Samantha said sadly.

"I hate to say it, but it could be possible," Nicholas agreed.

"Thank you for your help, Nicholas," Samantha smiled.

"Just remember you didn't hear any of it from me," Nicholas said firmly. He shook Eddy's hand as they stood to leave. "And don't forget about that lunch, Samantha."

"I won't," she promised.

# Chapter Nine

As Eddie and Samantha left Nicholas' office to head back to Sage Gardens Eddy's phone rang.

"It's Walt," he said as he answered the phone. "Walt, did you find something?"

"I sure did. Mike is in debt, a lot of debt. His mortgage is behind, his car is on the verge of being repossessed and he has quite a few outstanding loans. I don't even want to tell you about the credit cards or the collection agencies."

"That doesn't sound good," Eddy said grimly. "We just found out that only last week James changed his will to leave everything to Mike."

"Oh wow, that certainly pins the spotlight right on Mike as our potential killer."

"Yes, it does," Eddy said. He hung up the phone and looked over at Samantha.

"Looks like Mike was in a ton of financial trouble."

After they returned to Sage Gardens they met with Walt at his house. As the three gathered around Walt's kitchen table they discussed the case. "So, sonny boy drops back into his life out of the blue," Eddy pointed out. "Convinces his Daddy Dearest to leave the money to him, and then suddenly James is in the ground. Dale the janitor I talked to said that he heard James and Mike fighting about money a few weeks ago. Maybe Mike got James to change the will, and then felt pressured to strike before James had the chance to change it again."

"That does make sense," Walt nodded. Then he grimaced. "I don't mean that it makes sense that he killed his father, but that he had motive to."

"Yes, and motive is what counts," Eddy said thoughtfully. "But what motive would he have to steal his own father's watch? Unless he wanted to sell it and claim it on insurance."

"I have someone looking into the watch situation," Samantha blurted out.

"You do?" Eddy arched an eyebrow. "Who?"

"I can't really say," Samantha said uncomfortably.

"What do you mean you can't say?" Eddy asked again. His investigative nature caused him to grow more interested.

"I mean, I promised her it would be our secret. She might be able to find out who stole the watch," Samantha explained nervously. She was beginning to regret saying anything about it. She knew just how skilled Eddy was at getting information out of people.

"Secrets?" Walt frowned. "I don't like secrets. Secrets lead to messes, and messes are not pleasant," he settled his gaze on Samantha as well. Samantha took a slight step back as both of the men focused in on her.

"If she finds anything, I'll let you know," she attempted to assure them both.

"You'll let us know," Eddy countered, his voice growing a little rougher.

"Excuse me?" Samantha shot back with annoyance. Before she could tell Eddy exactly how she felt about his comment, her cell phone began to ring. She glowered at him and fished her phone out of her purse. She didn't recognize the number, but was happy for the distraction. "Hello?" she asked hesitantly.

"Sam, it's Jo," Jo said swiftly.

Samantha looked from Eddy to Walt, and then lowered her eyes. She turned away from the two men.

"Did you find something?" she asked hopefully.

"I have a lead," Jo replied suspiciously. "Why are you talking so softly?"

"I'm with my friends," Samantha explained quietly. "You can tell me if you found something."

"This is supposed to be our secret, remember?" Jo said sharply. "You didn't tell anyone did you?"

"No," Samantha cleared her throat. "But I

might need to."

"Why would you need to?" Jo asked incredulously. "I don't want you telling anyone."

"Because we're acting as a team," Samantha frowned.

"This is ridiculous," Jo muttered. "I just need a description of the watch so that I can make sure I have the right fence."

"Oh, a description of the watch?" Samantha repeated.

"Who is that?" Eddy asked.

"Is that your secret friend?" Walt questioned and stood up from the computer chair.

"Who is that in the background?" Jo demanded.

"Jo, are you going to see the fence today?" Samantha asked quickly.

"No, I can't go until tomorrow," Jo replied shortly.

"Let's meet tomorrow then. I'll give you the

description of the watch tomorrow," Samantha rushed to say.

"What? Why?" Jo asked, just as Samantha was hanging up the phone.

She tucked her phone back into her purse and looked up at the two men who were still staring at her curiously. All three were silent for a few moments.

"Well?" Walt finally asked.

"Well what?" Samantha asked in return.

"Well, who was that on the phone?" Walt asked.

"A friend," she replied and lowered her eyes again.

"Enough of this," Eddy snapped. "I know exactly who she was talking to."

"You do?" Samantha asked with surprise and some guilt.

"Sure," he narrowed his eyes. "You said her name Jo."

"I did not!" Samantha growled.

"Oh, that's right she did," Walt said and snapped his fingers sharply.

"I didn't realize," Samantha said with a frown.

"So, who is this Jo?" Eddy demanded.

"Well, there's a Jo that lives here in Sage Gardens," Walt pointed out. "She moved in not that long ago."

"You know her?" Samantha asked.

"Oh no, not really," Walt said shyly. "I just noticed her and overheard her name."

"Who is she?" Eddy asked as he locked eyes with Samantha. "I know I know her from somewhere."

"Uh, well," Samantha felt a ripple of tension rise up along her spine. She knew that she had already revealed too much.

"Listen Sam, doing something like this, conducting an investigation like this, requires a certain amount of trust," Eddy said gravely. "I want to know the truth. If you can't trust me with it, then we don't have any business doing this."

"Don't say that, Eddy," Samantha said with a frown. "It's not that I don't trust you. It's not like that. It's just that she asked that I respect her privacy."

"I'm going to find out either way," Eddy pointed out. "Either I ask you who she is, or I ask her."

"You wouldn't do that, would you?" Samantha asked apprehensively. "I wasn't supposed to tell anyone who she is."

"I would, and I will," he replied sternly. "She talks to me like she knows me. I need to know who she is."

"She spoke to you?" Samantha asked.

"Yes, she did," he replied and narrowed his eyes. "Now, out with it."

"Samantha, we're your friends," Walt said in a gentler tone. "You can tell us the truth."

Samantha took a shaky breath. "All right," she finally conceded. "But you both have to promise not to tell anyone else. Especially you, Eddy," she said and looked directly into his eyes.

"Tell us," Eddy said without agreeing.

"Jo, the woman that lives here in Sage Gardens, is Joanne Baylor, the same woman who..."

"The cat burglar?" Eddy asked with disbelief.

"The what?" Walt stammered out.

"Yes, the cat burglar," Samantha finally admitted and felt as if a big burden had been lifted off her shoulders, only to be replaced by the dread of Jo finding out that she had told her secret.

"This is absolutely ridiculous," Eddy growled. "How could you even associate with that woman, Samantha? How does she have your phone number?"

"Listen, she offered to help, and what better way to catch a thief, than to use a thief?" Samantha explained quickly.

"No, don't you even try it," Eddy warned her. "There is no explanation for this, and you know it.

She's a dangerous criminal who will say and do anything to get what she wants."

"She's done her time, Eddy," Samantha pointed out, though she didn't fully believe it herself. "She was released early for good behavior. She offered to help because she wants to turn her life around."

"I'll believe that when pigs fly," Eddy snapped and shook his head. "Walt, are you buying any of this?"

"I don't know," Walt replied with a slight frown. "She has a point about a thief catching a thief. Hopefully Jo will be able to help."

"I can't even conceive of what the two of you are thinking," Eddy said sharply. Then he stormed out of Walt's villa.

"Eddy, wait!" Samantha called out and started to follow after him. Walt grasped her arm gently and held her back.

"Let him go," he advised. "He needs a little time to cool off."

Samantha frowned and looked down at the floor. She knew that she was the reason that Eddy was so upset. Even with everything that was going on, she didn't want Eddy to be angry with her. She wondered if he might be right, that she had made the wrong choice by allowing Jo to be involved.

***

Eddy did his best to calm down. There was little that bothered him more than a criminal who was given back their freedom before they had served all of their sentence. He didn't really believe that people could change. The idea that an infamous cat burglar had been living in the same community as him, had even spoken to him, without him realizing made it very difficult for him. Had he really gotten so rusty that a criminal could flaunt herself right under his nose?

He didn't want to be at his villa if one of them came looking for him, so he walked down towards the lake. His mind was still churning over the case as well. Jo was a distraction, but he needed to focus on what mattered. If Mike was responsible for his father's death then he needed to suffer severe consequence for it. The only thing that bothered him was how obvious it seemed.

"I thought I might find you out here," Samantha said quietly as she stepped up behind him. Eddy tensed, but he did not turn away from the water to face her.

"You shouldn't sneak up on an old detective," he muttered and slid his hands into his pockets.

"I wasn't sneaking," Samantha insisted as she moved around beside him. "I just didn't want to disturb you," she explained.

"Oh?" he glanced over at her and raised an eyebrow. "I'm fairly disturbed now, aren't I?"

"Eddy, don't you ever just relax?" Samantha asked as she narrowed her eyes. "Does everything have to be an argument, or an interrogation?"

"I was trying to relax," Eddy pointed out. "I was looking out over the water. I was calm, and quiet. Then you showed up," he looked over at her once more, his expression indifferent.

"All right, I get the point, I'll go," Samantha said with a sigh of frustration. She grasped the pole on the canopy and began to swing around it to walk away.

"Wait, don't go," Eddy said sternly. "I'm sorry, I was just kidding around."

"That's kidding around?" she asked with widened eyes as she looked back at him. "I guess I missed the humor."

"I guess you did," he admitted sheepishly. "I've been a little rough around the edges today."

"Because of Jo?" Samantha asked and searched his expression for a hint of the truth. He grimaced.

"Maybe," he said quietly. "I'm not sure how to feel about working with someone so notorious."

"We all have our pasts, Eddy," Samantha reminded him as she leaned against the pole of the canopy and looked out over the water. "There are choices that we've made that we will be dealing with for the rest of our lives. But Jo paid her debt, didn't she?"

"Not exactly," Eddy replied with a scowl. "There were a lot more robberies that didn't get connected to her. I'm sure she's responsible for at least a few of them. However, she only went to jail for a handful that could actually be proven. That's why she got out as early as she did, Samantha. Am I just supposed to ignore the way she broke the law and be buddies with her now?"

"No one is asking you to do that, Eddy," Samantha assured him. "You think that everything is black and white. Not everything is. Did Jo commit crimes? Yes, she did," Samantha nodded. "You and I both know that. But what is the point of a criminal doing their best to change their ways if they are never given the opportunity to turn their lives around?"

"I don't know, Sam," he shook his head and looked away from her again. "It goes against my better judgment. I don't think we should trust her."

"Who ever said anything about trusting her?" Samantha asked with a slight smile. "It's not as if I expect you to do that."

"So, why are you asking her for help?"

"For James' sake," she explained. "If involving her leads to finding the watch and possibly the murderer then it's worth it."

"It sounded like you were going to let her handle talking to the fence alone," Eddy said.

"It might have sounded that way, but I'm not going to let her do that," Samantha replied. "Why do you think I told her to meet me tomorrow so I could give her a description of the watch?"

"You intend to go with her?" Eddy asked suspiciously.

"I'm not some kind of delicate flower, Eddy. No, I didn't wear a badge, but I did conduct my own investigations. I haven't forgotten how to do just that," she insisted sternly.

"You're not going with her," Eddy said as if his

words ended the discussion.

"Fine," Samantha said. She smiled at the surprised look on his face. "But someone has to go with her. So, if it's not me, then I guess it's going to have to be you."

"Me?" he asked and shook his head. "I don't think I could keep my cool. I'd want to slap handcuffs on her."

Samantha struggled not to point out how his comment might be taken by anyone else who heard it. "You don't have handcuffs anymore," she reminded him. "Besides, the best way to deal with a problem is to face it. Right?"

"I don't know," he shook his head hesitantly. "It just doesn't seem like a very good idea for me to get in the middle of all of that."

"Well, like I said, it's me or you," Samantha shrugged. "I was already planning on joining her, so it's not going to be a problem for me to stick with that plan."

"Samantha, you know better than that," he

said sharply. "The things that can happen are innumerable. Undercover situations are always unpredictable, and we're talking about real criminals here, with real guns. Not, an article that you're writing."

"I am perfectly aware of what we're talking about," Samantha said evenly. "My offer still stands. I'll be happy to avoid putting myself at risk if you would prefer to do the honors."

"Oh, Sam," he sighed and closed his eyes briefly. "My life used to be simple you know."

"I highly doubt that," Samantha chuckled. "I'll have her meet us around ten in the morning."

"Fine," he reluctantly agreed. "I'll be there."

"Eddy, just do your best to think of Jo as an asset," Samantha suggested. "She really could make a difference in solving the murder."

"We'll see," Eddy replied before turning back towards his villa. As Samantha turned back towards the water she caught the reflection of the sun sparkling along the surface. It reminded her of the champagne they had been drinking not long ago at James' party. She frowned.

"We're fighting to find out the truth," she said quietly.

# Chapter Ten

The next morning Eddy woke up surly. He thought about not meeting Samantha and Jo. He didn't want to have anything to do with the criminal. On the other hand he did very much want to find out the truth and bring James' killer to justice. Finding out who stole the watch could bring him one step closer to making that happen. Reluctantly, he forced himself out of bed and into the shower.

Everything in his villa had an army green feel, despite the fact that he had never been in the army. The color made him feel at peace in his environment. Even his shower curtain was army green. He kept his shelves bare of anything other than necessities and a few very well read books. When he emerged from the shower he was wrapped in an army green towel. He snatched a pair of slacks from his closet, paired it with a button-down shirt, and a brown suit jacket, then dressed. He paused in front of the mirror only to adjust his hat on the top of his head.

As Eddy was walking down towards Samantha's villa, he received a text on his cell phone.

*Meet us by the lake. Act like you don't know anything.*

Eddy raised an eyebrow at the message, which had come from Samantha's phone. He put his phone away and changed direction to walk towards the lake. He could see the pair already standing there, deep in discussion.

"I'm just not comfortable with you going alone," Samantha explained as Eddy walked up behind the two of them.

"Who would go with me? You?" Jo laughed at the idea. Her laughter faded when Eddy spoke.

"What's going on here?" he asked.

Jo looked over her shoulder at him with a mixture of hatred and curiosity.

"It's a private conversation," she replied shortly.

"Between a crime journalist and a criminal, seems like a bad idea," Eddy said casually. Samantha glared at him. Eddy pretended not to notice.

"Jo said she has some contacts that might be able to tell us who fenced the watch," Samantha explained as she looked nervously over at Eddy.

"She's standing right here, can't she tell me that?" he asked as he continued to stare steadily at Jo.

"I wasn't sure that you'd be interested in listening," Jo countered in an even tone. She was doing her best not to show that Eddy's presence made her uneasy. She knew that she was failing miserably.

"Well, how do you know unless you ask?" Eddy replied in an almost identical tone.

"The point is, that she is offering to help," Samantha explained in an attempt to keep them both calm. "She's going to check into her connections and see what she can find out."

"Or, she's going to cover up for the fact that she's involved in all of this," Eddy accused.

"I already have a meeting lined up," Jo replied in a sharp tone. "I'm going to meet a fence now who I think might have the watch. If you want to tag along, fine."

"Let's get one thing clear, I don't tag along with anyone," Eddy said and shook his head. He glanced over at Samantha briefly. Samantha cringed. She didn't think that the two of them would survive being alone in a car together.

"I'm leaving," Jo said and muttered something under her breath about ever getting involved.

"We'll take my car," Eddy said firmly. As the two walked towards the parking lot Walt walked up to Samantha.

"Where are they going?" he asked with confusion.

"Jo set up a meeting with the fence she thinks bought the watch from whoever stole it," Samantha explained. "And Eddy is going with her."

"Oh," Walt frowned. "That doesn't seem like a very good idea."

"No Walt, it really doesn't," Samantha agreed. The sound of Eddy gunning the engine punctuated her words.

***

As Eddy steered the car out of the parking lot and onto the road, he could tell that Jo was as uncomfortable as he was. The truth was he had worked with several criminal informants in the past. He was familiar with what it was like to be alone with a felon. However, Jo was different. She had led detectives on a wild goose chase as they searched for her. She was cunning, and manipulative, and Eddy wasn't going to take his eye off her for a second.

"Head to Newton," Jo instructed him, though she did not turn to look at him. The sharp click of the turn signal switch was the only sound that filled the car. Eddy turned down the highway in the direction of Newton and did his best to keep his focus on the road instead of on Jo.

"I guess you know exactly who I am," Jo suddenly said. She was still staring steadily out of the passenger door window.

Eddy hesitated a moment and then nodded. "I know who you are," he replied.

"And I know exactly who you are," Jo sighed and sank down in the seat. Eddy noticed that she slouched elegantly. She didn't try to hide her body, or communicate a lack of pride, it was more like she was relaxing.

"You do?" Eddy asked. "Why would you know anything about me?"

"I knew a lot about a lot of people that live in Sage Gardens even before I moved in," Jo admitted. "Turn right up here, on Kent."

Eddy glanced over at her curiously. Then he slowed down to make the right turn. Once they were on Kent he cleared his throat.

"How do you know so much about the residents?" he asked.

"I knew that no matter what place I picked to live, there was going to be someone who knew something about me. I mean with the burglaries in the paper, it's hard to avoid. However, I was hoping to avoid places that would specifically have people that would cause me trouble," she looked at him out of the corner of her eye. "Guess I made a bad choice."

"I thought you said you knew a lot about us before you moved in?" Eddy frowned.

"I did, however I didn't really look that deep. I didn't realize you were a retired cop until I had already signed the lease. Then there was Samantha, whose name I would have recognized if she hadn't written all of those articles about me under a pen name," she sneered with frustration.

"You read the articles?" he asked.

"Yes, I had a good amount of free time in prison you know," she sighed. "Up here on the left we can pull in, then you're going to want to drive through the parking lot into the next plaza."

"Seems like you know this place fairly well," Eddy observed.

"Well, you know what they say," she shrugged.

"No? What?" he asked and parked the car.

"Keep your enemies close," she reminded him. "It's hard to survive in this world as a felon without friends."

"I don't know that you should be considering known criminals, friends," Eddy pointed out as he tucked his keys into his pocket.

"They're the only ones I have," Jo replied darkly. She opened the door to the car and stepped out into the parking lot. The business they were parked in front of barely had a sign. The windows were streaked with dirt. Crumpled up papers and leaves littered the sidewalk.

"This is the place?" Eddy asked as he stepped up beside her.

"Yes," she replied. "I think it might be best if you wait out here," Jo said as she lingered by the door. The glass was covered with various stickers and sale signs.

"I don't think so," Eddy said gruffly as he stood between her and the door.

"You still don't trust me?" she asked.

"Did I say that?" he asked and met her eyes.

"You didn't have to," she replied gravely as she studied him. "It's written all over your face."

"You may think that's what I mean, but it's not what I mean," Eddy said with frustration. "I'm not going to let you go into a place where a known criminal does business, alone."

"You think that you are going to protect me?" she asked with a smirk. "How sweet."

"I just think it's best that you don't go alone," he corrected her sternly.

"Fine," she nodded. "You can come in with me, but you have to stop acting all cop-ish."

"Cop-ish?" he repeated. "I've worked undercover before."

"And I'm sure you were an easy mark," she sighed and swept her eyes over him. "First you have to lose the hat, it just screams cop on you. On me, it'll be fine," she plucked his hat off his head and dropped it on hers. Carefully she tucked her dark hair back behind her ears. Eddy stared at her with disbelief.

Before he could say a word she ran her hands back through his light brown hair. He shuddered at the sudden touch.

"Relax cowboy, I'm just fixing your hat hair," she frowned and smoothed his hair back until it looked slick.

"Stop," he said with annoyance. "That's enough."

"Not quite yet," she replied and grabbed the collar of his dress shirt. She unbuttoned the top two buttons. Eddy shifted uncomfortably but he didn't push her hand away. "Let's let that shirt loose," she said.

"I'll do that," he said sharply and pulled out his own shirt. He straightened his belt and then sighed. "All right, do I look enough like a criminal for you?" he asked.

Jo studied him critically. "Maybe if you scowled a little less," she suggested.

"I don't think that's possible," he muttered.

"I actually believe that," she replied with a slight shake of her head. "Okay, now let me do all of the talking. Understand?"

"Whatever you say," he said grimly. He jerked the door of the pawn shop open and held it open for Jo to walk through. Jo adjusted his hat on her head and winked lightly at him before she walked inside the shop. Eddy followed after her. The interior was fairly dim, which was a big tip off that it was not a legitimate business. Most pawn shops would be well lit and showcasing their electronics and jewelry. In this one he had to strain to see any of the items, and most of the items were not very valuable.

"Roger," she called out as she walked further into the pawn shop.

"Jo?" a voice called back from beyond the counter. A burly man stepped out from behind a drab curtain. He smiled at Jo, but his smile faded when he saw Eddy standing behind her.

"I brought a friend, the one that was interested in that watch," Jo explained.

"I don't like friends," he said darkly and glared openly at Eddy.

"Don't worry, pal, I'm not any competition," Eddy said casually. "I don't have a lot of time, do you have what I need or not?"

"Yes," he said and continued to study Eddy with clear disapproval. "You can come back with me, Jo, but he needs to stay out here."

"I don't think so," Eddy said sharply. "I don't trust this one any more than I trust you. How do I know you won't be switching out the watch while

I'm not looking?"

"Hmm," Roger shook his head slowly. "I don't know where you find these people, Jo," he sighed. "Fine, come on back. Let's get this over with."

He turned and walked back behind the curtain. Jo shot Eddy a brief glare, then she followed after Roger. Eddy stayed right behind her. The back room was filled with neatly stacked boxes and wire shelving ran the length of the walls.

"Here it is," Roger said when he pulled down a small box. "Now," he turned to face Eddy with a grim stare. "This isn't the exact watch that you asked for."

"What?" Eddy asked with displeasure. "You said you had the watch."

"I did have the watch, but not anymore," Roger explained. "I sold it almost right away. But, I have a similar watch that I'm willing to offer you."

"I don't want a similar watch," Eddy snapped.

Jo placed her hand lightly on his arm to calm him.

"Listen Roger, it isn't so much the watch that we're interested in. We want to know who sold it to you," she tilted her head a little and smiled seductively at the man. "Do you think that's something that you could tell us?"

"Why would I?" he asked in a low growl. "I knew that you were up to something, Jo. I don't hear from you when you get out of the clink, and now you're calling in favors. What is this really about?"

"The watch belonged to a good friend of mine," Eddy interrupted. "It has sentimental value. I want to find out who stole it so I can pound the life out of them."

"Oh," Roger laughed a little. "Well, I guess that makes more sense. Hmm," he reached up and scratched at his cheek where a few pimples resided amidst stubble. "Well, I didn't catch his name, but I can tell you he has a tattoo on his arm. A snake."

"You really can't tell us anything else?" Jo

pressed.

"He doesn't need to," Eddy said gravely. "I know exactly who it was. Thanks for your time," he nodded at Roger and then started to walk away.

"Wait just a minute," Roger said. "I don't want you causing any trouble on my account," he growled.

"Too late," Eddy cast his words over his shoulder. He gestured to Jo to join him. Jo hesitated for a moment as if she might want to smooth things over with Roger, then reluctantly she followed after Eddy. As soon as they were outside she turned to face him.

"What was that?" she demanded.

"What?" Eddy asked innocently and unlocked the doors to the car.

"You know exactly what," Jo said with impatience. "I told you not to act like a cop. Now Roger is going to know that I associate with the police."

Eddy leaned against the top of the car, his eyes locked on Jo's. He let her words hang in the air for a moment before he spoke.

"I'm not the police," he said calmly. "Even if I was, I thought you were ready to turn your life around, Joanne? Why would you care what a criminal thinks of you?"

Jo glared at him and jerked open the passenger side door. She ignored him as she settled into the seat. Eddy afforded her silence, and she did the same, and started the engine. He knew he had ruffled her feathers. As he drove back towards Sage Gardens she continued to fume. After a few minutes the tension seemed to subside.

"Who do you think it was that stole the watch?" she asked.

He didn't look in her direction. "That's not really your concern, is it?"

"I helped you find out who it was, didn't I?" she shot a look of animosity towards him. Eddy continued to stare out through the windshield.

"You did your part," he said evenly as he pulled into Sage Gardens. "Now, I'll do mine."

"What are you going to do?" Jo asked as she stepped out of the car.

"Never mind that," Eddy shrugged off her attention and began walking away from the car.

"Wait, maybe I can help," Jo offered as she quickened her pace to catch up with him.

"Oh, you're feeling particularly charitable today?" he asked and glanced over at her with distaste. "You've done enough."

"Apparently not," Jo shot back with obvious frustration. "You don't seem to be giving me any credit for it."

"Credit?" he retorted. "You're lucky I don't turn you into the police."

"I didn't do anything wrong," Jo growled.

"You associated with a known criminal," Eddy pointed out with a mild shrug. "With my say so, you could end up back in jail for quite a bit longer than you have left to live."

"You really are a jerk, you know that?" Jo snapped. "Forget it. I knew that I was making a mistake when I offered to help. None of your kind will ever see me as anything but a criminal no matter what I do."

"What do you care?" he questioned roughly.

"I don't," she shook her head and stomped away.

Eddy turned and walked across the main square towards the main office. When he reached the door he was relieved to find it unlocked. He pushed the door open.

"Where's Dale?" he asked the woman who was sitting behind the desk. He didn't recognize her, but that didn't surprise him, as the owners had been using temporary workers lately.

"I think he's cleaning 32," the woman replied slowly as if she wasn't sure if she should be giving him the information.

Eddy didn't wait to hear another word from her. He turned and walked out of the office. He walked straight towards the villa where Dale should have been working. He spotted the small, white golf cart parked outside the villa stocked with an assortment of cleaning products. Eddy walked quietly up to the door of the villa which was propped open. He paused just outside the door and looked inside. He could hear Dale moving around inside.

"I need to speak to you," he said sternly.

He heard something hit the ground. "Dale," Eddy said again sharply. "I need to speak with you."

Dale reluctantly walked up to the door.

"What?" he asked with defiance.

"I know what you did," Eddy growled.

"What are you talking about?" Dale demanded and started to back up further into the house.

"I know you stole his watch, did you poison him, too?" Eddy barked out.

"Poison? Are you crazy?" Dale's voice rose.

"You have no idea what you're saying."

"I know exactly what I'm saying," Eddy shot back and grabbed Dale by the wrist. He jerked his wrist until his arm was straight, revealing the snake tattoo that was hiding beneath the sleeve of his shirt.

"The fence identified you, Dale," Eddy explained as Dale yanked his wrist out of Eddy's grasp.

"All right, all right," Dale grimaced. "Really, it was a victimless crime. You know the pay here is nothing," Dale said dismissively. "I can't survive on it. I knew how loaded James was. He would always brag to me about it while I was cleaning his villa. He liked to talk about how he could buy and sell the entire Sage Gardens if he wanted to."

"And?" Eddy asked as he stared at the young man incredulously.

"And, when he died, I just," he frowned and shook his head. "I mean it wasn't like he was going to miss it. Right?"

"Dale," Eddy sighed. His lips drew into a thin line of disappointment as he studied the young man. "You stole it?"

"I took it," Dale corrected him. "I mean, James liked me. If he had known he was going to die, he might have given me the watch."

"But he didn't," Eddy said sharply. "He didn't give anything to you. You stole it."

"Have you ever been in my shoes?" Dale demanded. "I have rent to pay. How am I supposed to do that with this dead-end job? I needed something to just get me by until next month. I don't think that's such a terrible thing."

"It is a terrible thing," Eddy snapped back. "I've been in your shoes, pal. I've worked my whole life, and I have never stolen from anyone. I always paid my bills on time, even if it meant I had to pull extra shifts or miss out on the things I wanted to do."

"Oh right, of course you did, back when rent was about a dollar a day," he waved his hand dismissively.

"A dollar a day?" Eddy growled in return. "Just how old do you think I am?"

"I don't care," Dale said and glared at Eddy. "The point is that you are never going to understand where I'm coming from."

"No, I'm not," Eddy replied gruffly. "Because I am not a thief."

"Are you sure about that?" Dale chuckled. "So high and mighty like you've never made a mistake in your life. I wasn't even the only one casing the room. Someone got there before me. He was leaving when I was walking up. So, it's not like I was the only one. Go ahead, call the cops on me, get me fired. What's the difference? My life isn't going anywhere."

"Maybe it would if you made an effort," Eddy challenged him. "I've made more mistakes than I care to recount, but I can tell you none of those mistakes ever led to me breaking the law. Instead, every time I messed up, I searched for a way to fix it. I learned, I grew, but I didn't steal."

"Whatever, spare me the lecture. Just do what

you have to do and get me locked up," Dale shook his head. Eddy pulled out his phone. He was just about to call the police, when he remembered what Jo had said to him. Keep your enemies close. Dale had admitted to stealing the watch. But that didn't make him a murderer. Slowly he slid his phone back into his pocket.

"All right, Dale, I'm going to give you a chance to make up for what you've done," Eddy said grimly.

"What?" Dale stared at him in shock. "What do I have to do?"

"All I want you to do is pay attention. Listen in on conversations. Notice who is coming and who is going. I don't think James died of a heart attack, I think someone poisoned him, and now to make up for you stealing his watch, you're going to help figure out who did it," Eddy said with confidence.

"I don't know," Dale hesitated. "I don't want to make a murderer angry."

"Well, the way I see it, Dale, you have two

choices. You can either make a murderer angry, or you can make me angry," Eddy raised his eyebrows. "Lock up is one phone call away."

"Fine," Dale sighed. "I'll do it. I'll find out what I can," he paused a moment and studied Eddy intently. "You're really not going to turn me in?"

"Not just yet," Eddy replied darkly. Then he walked away.

# Chapter Eleven

When Eddy got back to his villa he had a decision to make. He could tell Samantha and Walt what he had learned about Dale, or he could keep it to himself. He was more than a little concerned that if he told them about Dale, they would want to have him arrested. Eddy knew that he should have him arrested. But he was hoping that Dale's desperation would prove to be valuable in the search for the murderer.

Eddy was just about to settle into bed to try to get some rest when his cell phone rang. He glanced at the ID on the screen and found that it was Owen.

"Hey, Owen," Eddy said as he answered the phone.

"Eddy, what's going on?" Owen asked with some urgency.

"Is something wrong, Owen?" Eddy asked and sat up in his bed.

"I heard from some of the staff that you've been tearing through the place, making demands," Owen said quickly. "The office girl was so upset that she asked me if I thought she should call the police."

"I may have been a little extra passionate," Eddy admitted. "I needed to find Dale. He's the one that stole James' watch."

"Did he kill James, too?" Owen asked with shock.

"I don't think so. But I'm hoping that he can help us find out who did," Eddy explained. "Anyway, I promise I won't scare the office lady anymore."

"Just be careful, Eddy," Owen said. "I know that you're used to this kind of thing, but the last time you investigated a crime it was with a badge and a gun. This is a different kind of situation."

"I'm realizing that," Eddy agreed. "Don't worry about me, Owen. I'll be just fine."

"Call me if you need anything," Owen

insisted.

"Thanks, Owen," Eddy said before hanging up the phone. It was nice for Eddy that Owen appeared to care about him. It seemed like a long time since someone had.

Eddy closed his eyes and began running through the case in his mind. When he finally fell asleep, his thoughts were still racing. Even in his sleep his mind was filled with thoughts about James. James at his party. James enjoying a toast with his son and the rest of the guests at the party. James raising a full glass of wine while everyone cheered. James drinking the entire glass in one swift gulp.

Eddy suddenly opened his eyes. He began to put two and two together. He remembered that there was a bottle of wine that James was drinking from that he did not share with anyone else at the party. All of the others who had something alcoholic to drink had champagne, or white wine, while James' drink was a dark, red wine that he kept with the rest of his gifts. With his heart pounding he picked up his phone. He dialed Samantha's number. She picked up after the third ring.

"Hello?" she asked with a yawn.

"Samantha, it's Eddy," he said.

"How early is it?" Samantha asked and groaned.

"Sorry, I just woke up and remembered something from the party. I wanted to see if you remembered it, too," he explained.

"Okay," she sighed and yawned again. "What was it?"

"James was drinking his own red wine," Eddy said.

"Yes," Samantha replied after thinking about it for a moment. "I do remember that."

"So, the wine could have been poisoned," Eddy rushed forward. "It might not have ever been the cupcake that was the murder weapon. It could have been the wine."

"The wine," Samantha repeated. "Where did

the wine come from?"

"That's what I don't know," Eddy replied. "I remember noticing the way that James hid it under the table his gifts were on, as if he didn't want to share. You would think he would offer someone a glass, at least his son."

"If he was being that greedy with it, then it was probably a favorite wine of his," Samantha pointed out. "Maybe it was a gift from someone who knew him quite well."

"Maybe," Eddy agreed. "But who?"

"I think we should go through the guest list. See if we can work out who gave him a gift and then talk to them," Samantha suggested.

"That will take quite some time," Eddy said as he shook his head. "Just about everyone at Sage Gardens was at that party."

"Then maybe we should start with those that were not from Sage Gardens," Samantha said thoughtfully. "Maybe even guests that showed up unexpectedly."

"Good idea," Eddy nodded.

"We'll get to the bottom of this," Samantha said.

"I think I might already have a lead," Eddy said with a small smile of realization.

"What lead?" Samantha asked curiously.

"I'll let you know if it pans out," Eddy replied. He hurried to dress and headed out of his villa. He thought about the promise he had made to Owen the night before, about being nicer to the staff. It was too late for that now. He hoped that Dale had seen and knew the man who walked out of James' room after he died. He wanted to know exactly who it was. With many of the staff just arriving for the day, it was easy to guess where Dale might be.

Eddy headed straight for the office. He carefully avoided being spotted by the office worker, as he knew that she might just call the police if she saw him. He saw a few staff members walking out from behind the office and guessed it was a gathering place for them before they started work for the day. He walked around the corner of the office to see if he could spot Dale. Eddy didn't have to look far to find Dale. All he had to do was follow the curl of smoke. It led him behind the dumpster. Dale was crouched down with a cigarette dangling from his lips. He appeared to be searching for something on the ground.

"Dale," Eddy said. Dale jumped at the sound of Eddy's authoritative voice.

"Oh no, not you again," Dale said with a sigh as he caught sight of Eddy. "Look, I've got nothing else to say to you. I haven't heard anything yet. No one is talking about anything other than the heart attack. You seem to be the only one with the crazy notion that James was poisoned."

"Never mind that," Eddy said. "That's not why I'm here."

"I've got nothing else to tell you," Dale insisted and stood up.

"That doesn't mean that I don't have some things to ask you," Eddy replied and narrowed his eyes. "You told me that when you slipped back into James' room, someone else was coming out right before you did. Who was it?"

"Uh," Dale frowned and glanced sideways to make sure that no one was close enough to hear him. "I'm not really sure what his name was. I think he's new around here. I know he's a resident, but I'm not sure where he lives."

"Lying to me again?" Eddy demanded as he moved closer to Dale.

"No way," Dale said swiftly. "You said you weren't going to turn me in, I'm not going to jerk you around."

"I said I wouldn't turn you in, as long as you mended your ways," Eddy corrected him. "So have you?"

"I'm working on it," Dale replied with some honesty. "I'm not lying to you. I don't know who the guy was."

"Did he have anything in his hands?" Eddy pressed. "You said it looked like he was stealing something, the last time I spoke to you. Did you see what it was?"

Dale closed his eyes for a moment as if he was trying to remember exactly what he had seen. When he opened them again, he nodded.

"Yes, I remember now," he frowned. "It was a bottle. Maybe a wine bottle."

"A wine bottle," Eddy repeated with disbelief. If the bottle of wine was poisoned then Dale had to be describing James' killer. "What did the guy look like?" Eddy asked eagerly.

"I don't know," Dale sighed. "I don't want to get in the middle of anything."

"Can't you remember anything about him?" Eddy demanded impatiently. Dale seemed to notice the shift in Eddy's demeanor and cleared his throat.

"All I know for sure was that I've seen him around since. I just don't know where he lives. I know where just about everyone around here lives. So, I'm guessing he's a fairly new resident," he lifted one shoulder in a half-shrug. "That's the best that I can do."

"I'm sure it is," Eddy replied with vague annoyance. "Just do me a favor, and no more stealing, okay?"

"Okay," Dale nodded. "If it keeps me out of jail, I'll stay on the straight and narrow."

"You do that," Eddy insisted.

As he walked away from Dale he dialed Samantha's number for the second time that morning. This time when she answered she sounded much more alert.

"Samantha, don't bother questioning any more of the guests," Eddy said in a rush as he walked quickly towards her villa. "I think I know who the killer is."

"You do?" Samantha asked with elation. "Who is it?"

"It's the new resident Frank," Eddy said sternly.

"Frank?" Samantha asked and then shook her head slightly. "I don't think that could be true. I spoke with Frank while we were at the party and after James died I checked to see he was okay."

"And?" Eddy asked. "Does that make him innocent?"

"Well no," Samantha said. She opened her door to find Eddy standing on her front porch. Eddy hung up his phone. Samantha hung up hers. "All I'm saying is that he didn't seem like a killer. Whatever was between Frank and James, James apologized for."

"Saying sorry doesn't always make it better," Eddy said grimly. "I think we need to figure out what exactly James was apologizing for, and whether it was worth murdering James over," Eddy said. "Dale, the guy who actually stole the watch said he saw Frank leaving James' room with a bottle of wine after he died."

"Then they wouldn't have found the wine in James' room," Samantha said with concern. "How do you know that your thief didn't also murder James? Maybe he thought he could get some good items from James' room if he was dead. Or maybe Mike even paid him to do it."

"I'm not saying that it's impossible," Eddy said and shook his head. "But we already know that there was some difficulty between James and Frank. I think getting to the bottom of that might give us a clearer idea of what happened."

"I can do that," Samantha offered. "Research is my specialty."

"Good," Eddy nodded and then glanced over at her. "Did you say you and Frank spoke a lot?"

"Not really," she replied with a mild shrug. "Like I said, he seemed nice enough."

"Murderers sometimes do," Eddy frowned. "Let me know what you find out. I'm going to see if Walt found out anything more from digging into the financials."

"Okay," Samantha nodded. "I'll update you."

"Good," Eddy started to turn towards the door and then stopped. He turned back to face Samantha.

"Have you heard anything from Jo?"

"Not since yesterday," Samantha said. "How

did you leave things with her?"

"Does it matter?" he asked. "She's a criminal."

"She was a criminal," Samantha corrected him.

"Really, Samantha?" Eddy asked and shook his head. "You know as well as I do that people don't just change like that."

"I know as well as you do that until you know someone's entire story, you don't know that person. Maybe there is more to Jo than you think," Samantha frowned. "She did help us out after all."

"Not without a price I'm sure," he said gravely.

"One of these days, Eddy, you're going to have to take a chance on someone," Samantha said knowingly. "I just hope that when you do, it's the right person."

"Is that another one of your riddles?" Eddy asked and raised an eyebrow.

"You'll see," Samantha said with confidence.

"I'm going to go to the library to look into things."

"All right, just be careful," Eddy said. "Right now Frank could be anywhere. If he's the killer, he might not like us sniffing into his past."

"I'll be careful," Samantha promised. Eddy nodded and then walked out of her villa. Samantha grabbed her purse and headed out as well.

# Chapter Twelve

The library had once been Samantha's favorite place. When she was a girl she would spend hours reading there. When she got older she would study there. When she started her career as a journalist she would often write at the library. It was a safe place to her, quiet and insulated, a place where she had never heard anyone raise their voice. As she settled into a seat in front of one of the computers, she knew that she could have done the research she needed to at home. But she preferred to be surrounded by the scent of books and the insulation of the library.

Samantha began looking into James' past. She wanted to find out how James and Frank's lives had converged in their past. As she was sorting through the information she could find on James year by year, she began to get to know the man even more. He had lived a mild but lonely life. She saw a marriage on record from when he was much younger and had ended after only five years. He had one son, Michael, with his wife. Samantha frowned as she sat back in her chair. She studied the information on the screen. She had heard of marriages breaking up quickly, but something about the timing of this marriage felt off. Why had James and his wife ended things when their child was only a few years old? Samantha managed to gain access to some information regarding the divorce. It was a contentious one, in which James was accused of infidelity.

"That was probably why Mike had a problem with him," Samantha said quietly and made a note in her notebook. "But it still doesn't explain where Frank comes in."

She decided to do some research on Frank during the same year that James divorced his wife. What she discovered was surprising. Frank had a record. He had been arrested on a domestic disturbance. However, the charges were later dropped.

"Interesting," Samantha said to herself with a

smirk.

Samantha placed a phone call to a friend in records at the police department.

"Martha, hi," she said when her friend answered. "I was wondering if you could give me some information about a domestic incident."

"Sure, but make it quick, I'm in the middle of a sea of paperwork," Martha replied dismally.

"I appreciate it, Martha," Samantha said.

"No problem, I'm sure it's for a groundbreaking article of yours," Martha said with warmth in her voice.

"I don't know how groundbreaking it will be, but it might just put a killer behind bars," Samantha offered in return.

"Hmm, well give me the case file number and the date, I will look it up right now," Martha said.

Samantha rattled off the information that Martha needed. Then she waited as Martha searched the records for the file.

"Oh wow, this is ancient," Martha said. "Okay,

the report states that it was a domestic incident. Apparently, Frank came home early from work and found his best friend James in bed with his wife. Frank was accused of physically assaulting James, and hurling furniture at his wife."

"Does it say why the charges were dropped?" Samantha asked curiously.

"It looks like both victims refused to press charges, and the prosecutor's office decided it wasn't worth pursuing," Martha replied. "You do realize that this happened over thirty years ago?"

"Yes," Samantha replied. "Sometimes old wounds still hurt."

"If there was ever a wound that would keep on hurting, this would be it," Martha sighed. "From the details of Frank's statement he was heartbroken and just lost his mind."

"I wonder if it's still lost," Samantha mused softly.

"Anything else you need?" Martha asked.

"I'll let you know," Samantha replied.

"Thanks, Martha."

"Anything for you, Sam," Martha said before hanging up the phone. Samantha hung up as well and sat back in the wooden chair. She stared at the picture on the screen of Frank as a young man. He was handsome then as well. She turned her attention back to James. She discovered that not only had James divorced his wife about the same time Frank divorced his, James had wasted no time re-marrying. Within a year he was legally married to Frank's ex-wife. Samantha cringed as she was sure that was a fairly good motive for Frank to kill James. She gathered her purse and shut down the website she had been using. She nodded to the librarian on her way out the door. When she reached the parking lot she dialed Eddy's number.

"We all need to get together and talk," she said. "I found some very interesting information."

"Walt's place?" Eddy suggested.

"I'll be there in ten minutes," Samantha replied before hanging up. As she started her car she wondered just how dangerous the ground was that she was treading on. If Frank was willing to kill James to get revenge, would he be willing to kill again to keep his secret?

*\*\**

Walt set three mugs of steaming tea down on the small dinette table in the corner of his kitchen. He made sure to place each one on a coaster on the table.

"Honey? Milk?" he offered as he looked between Eddy and Samantha.

"No, thank you," Eddy said.

"A little honey please," Samantha requested with a smile. Once they were settled around the table Samantha shared with Eddy and Walt the details that she had discovered.

"With the history that James and Frank shared, it would not surprise me that Frank murdered him," Samantha said before taking a sip of her tea.

"Let's make sure we're not getting ahead of ourselves," Eddy said and tapped the table top sharply with his pointer finger. "It's easy to get caught up in the momentum of things and jump to the wrong conclusion."

"You're right, just because it adds up doesn't mean that it's correct. We know that James had an affair with Frank's wife, and then married her," Walt said with a grave frown.

"We also know that James apologized to Frank the moment he saw him," Samantha added. "Which means that the wound between them had festered for over thirty years. James must have been carrying that guilt if he was so quick to apologize."

"And, it appears that James and Frank were best friends prior to the affair," Eddy sighed. "So, there was obviously a lot of emotional damage. That kind of emotional damage led to Frank getting charged with domestic violence."

"But the charges were dropped," Samantha

reminded him. "So, it can be assumed that James and Frank's wife, feeling guilty for what they did, decided not to make it worse by pressing charges."

"However, within a year they added insult to injury by getting married to each other," Walt said with mild disgust. "That doesn't sound like friendship to me."

"They must have really been in love," Samantha said thoughtfully.

"Being in love doesn't excuse betrayal," Walt said sharply. Samantha glanced up at him with surprise. He rarely spoke to her in such a tone. Eddy noticed it too and grimaced.

"It may not excuse it, but it happened," Eddy said calmly, hoping to discharge the tension. "So, we now have a pretty strong motive on Frank's part."

"But, wait a minute," Samantha said. "The only motive for Frank to kill James was the affair. But that took place over thirty years ago. Crimes of passion usually happen within the first twenty-four hours of the betrayal, not thirty years later."

"That's a good point," Eddy nodded.

"Betrayal can hurt the same years later," Walt argued. "I think it's possible that Frank was still angry and decided to take his revenge."

"But there's still Mike," Samantha pointed out. "Really, Frank wasn't the only person that James betrayed. He also cheated on his wife, and caused his family to be torn apart. Mike was only a young child when it happened, but it may have left a lasting impression on him. Perhaps he wanted to get revenge for the hurt his mother suffered, or maybe because James wasn't part of his life for so long."

"That's true," Eddy muttered.

"And Mike had the most to gain from killing James," Walt reminded them. "He stood to inherit a fortune, while Frank wouldn't get a dime."

"Of course there's always the chance that it was someone else entirely or that it wasn't even a murder," Samantha added with a sigh. "This is like getting stuck in a revolving door. Without any real, solid evidence we have no real direction to go in," she shook her head. "Maybe we should just take a break from the case for a little while. Give us time to think outside the box. Whenever I get stuck on an article I walk away for an hour or two, or even the day, to give my brain a chance to process. Usually it helps my focus to loosen up enough that I can think more clearly."

"That's a good idea," Eddy agreed. "We're not going to solve this today. To be honest, until we find some other clue, we're not going to be doing anything other than going around in circles."

"I could use a break from it," Walt admitted and drew a deep breath. "You two are used to this kind of thing, but this is my first murder investigation."

"All right, then it's agreed," Eddy said. "We'll all take a break from it this afternoon. Tomorrow, I'll see if I can get an update from the medical examiner. Maybe if we can find out what kind of poison was used we can pinpoint who recently purchased it."

"Okay," Walt nodded. "Do you think they'll open an investigation if the results come back positive for poison?"

"I know they will," Eddy replied. "Once they do it may be completely out of our hands. Detectives have rules and guidelines that they have to follow, or the case can be thrown out."

"So, whatever dirt we can get on Frank, we need to get it now," Samantha said with some urgency. "Maybe a break isn't such a good idea."

"Then what do you propose?" Walt asked curiously.

"Well," Samantha frowned. "I guess we need to find out if Frank gave James the bottle of wine."

"If he did, and he went to the trouble of stealing the bottle back after James was dead, then he might have kept the bottle," Eddy said with mounting excitement. "If we find that bottle we'll be able to prove that Frank was the one who poisoned James. There will probably be trace amounts of poison left in the bottle."

"I didn't notice it when I was in his villa," Samantha said thoughtfully.

"You were in his villa?" Eddy asked with surprise.

"Yes, when I spoke to him after the party, I just wanted to make sure he was okay," Samantha explained. "You know I was good friends with the man, Baki, who used to live there, so I helped with his trashcan because it always gets stuck. Oh!" Samantha's eyes suddenly widened.

"What?" Walt asked. Eddy leaned forward to listen.

"I kept slamming the trashcan to get it to go into the cabinet the way it should, and when I did I heard a bottle clanging. I thought it was beer bottles, because there were some missing from the six pack in his fridge. But he got upset with me for trying to help. On my way out I noticed there were empty beer bottles on the table. Maybe it was the wine bottle in the trashcan?"

"That's quite observant of you," Walt said with admiration.

"I always try to pay attention to small things," Samantha explained. "It can make the biggest difference in an article."

"Yes, to an investigation as well," Eddy agreed. "Do you really think the wine bottle was in there?"

"That might explain why it wouldn't close," Samantha said thoughtfully. "Usually it gets stuck on the track, but this time it was like something was blocking it. The wine bottle might have been too large for the small trashcan."

"Maybe it got wedged," Eddy nodded.

"Do you think it's still there?" Walt wondered out loud.

"Well, there's one way to know for sure," Eddy pointed out as he sat back on the wooden chair.

"What way is that?" Walt questioned, obviously intrigued.

Samantha looked over at Eddy curiously.

"We break in, and we find the bottle," Eddy uttered gravely. "If it's there, we have our proof, if it's not, we might at least find the poison that he used to kill James."

"You can't be serious," Walt said and raised a thin eyebrow. "You're talking about breaking and entering, Eddy. You of all people should have respect for the law."

"I have plenty of respect for the law," Eddy replied and snapped his eyes towards Walt with an offended expression. "I have zero respect for murderers. If Frank is responsible for James' death, I'm not going to let the law be the reason why he gets away with it."

"I disagree," Walt said sharply. "We don't even know if he's the murderer or even if James was murdered for sure. I won't be involved in it. Don't even think about me breaking into anywhere."

"I didn't ask you to do it, did I?" Eddy countered, his voice raising with frustration.

Samantha's words cut through the heat of the moment. "I know someone who can," she said quietly, but with a tinge of excitement in her voice.

"What?" both men asked as they looked over at Samantha with surprise.

"Not me," she said swiftly. "I mean, I don't think I'd be very good at it," she explained. "But I do know someone who would be perfect for the job."

"You know someone who would make a perfect thief?" Eddy asked with disbelief. "Are you talking about Jo?"

"One of the best thieves I have ever known," Samantha explained with a pleased smile.

"Now you're talking about encouraging a reformed felon to re-offend?" Walt demanded incredulously.

"We don't know that she's reformed," Eddy reminded them. "We still don't even know for sure that she didn't have anything to do with this."

"Oh please, Eddy, why would she want to kill James?" Samantha asked and shook her head.

"Maybe he found out about her secret," Eddy suggested. "Maybe she panicked and decided to get rid of him."

"She's a thief not a murderer," Samantha replied with shock.

"It's a slippery slope, Sam," Eddy said and drank some of his tea.

"Not Jo, Eddy. I studied her. She was a cat burglar, one of the best. But she never harmed a hair on anyone's head. Even that one time when a museum guard stumbled onto her, she went out of her way to make her escape without harming him," she reminded Eddy.

"I guess that makes her a saint?" Eddy asked and raised an eyebrow.

"I didn't say that, but I don't think it's fair to make her seem like a serial killer," Samantha argued in return.

"I think you're underestimating Jo. She had detectives in knots over how to catch her. Everyone knew who she was, but no one could prove it," he chuckled a little and shook his head. "Detectives lost a lot of sleep over her."

"Like I said, she did her time," Samantha said sternly.

"There's one problem," Walt said grimly. "You said you know her, but you don't really. She was reluctant to even help us find the fence. Do you really think she would help with something like this? You're asking her to risk everything, including her freedom."

"It can't hurt to ask, can it?" Samantha smiled a little.

"It can if she isn't trustworthy," Eddy said and narrowed his eyes.

"I can't believe that we've been living in Sage Gardens with a murderer and a thief," Walt shook his head. "Secure environment the pamphlet said. I knew I should have gotten that second deadbolt."

"Relax," Samantha rolled her eyes. "You don't have anything she's interested in I'm sure."

"Maybe not, but maybe James did," Eddy said with narrowed eyes. "Maybe Jo had an angle on getting his fortune. Maybe Mike even hired her to make all of this look like an accident."

"Are we back on this?" Samantha growled. "Eddy, seriously. She helped us find out who stole the watch."

"Who they claimed stole the watch," Eddy argued sharply. "It could all be part of her plan."

"Wow, you are paranoid," Samantha shook her head. "I really don't think that Jo is part of some vast conspiracy."

"You have to look at it from all angles," Eddy warned her. "Right now we believe that Frank might be the killer, but we don't have any more proof that he is, than we do that Jo is."

"So, let's get some," Samantha said with confidence. "If Jo's game then I think we should do it. The longer we wait, the bigger chance there is that Frank will get rid of the evidence. If he hasn't already."

"I don't know," Walt hesitated. "This is really treading in dangerous waters."

"Illegal waters," Eddy growled. "And don't think that Jo wouldn't sell us all out in a second if she gets caught."

"Sometimes you have to have a little faith in people, Eddy," Samantha said and gave him a light pat on his shoulder. "I'll go talk to her, you drink more tea and calm down."

"I'm calm," Eddy barked.

"Tea," Samantha said and pointed to his half-empty cup. "He may need a refill, Walt. Let's meet in an hour down by the lake," she suggested.

"We'll be there," Walt said. "Just remember she's still a criminal."

"I'll be fine," Samantha assured them both before she walked out of the villa.

# Chapter Thirteen

Samantha stopped at her place to pick up a box of muffins she had bought. In her experience it was always better not to show up empty handed when she was asking someone to do something for her. Once she was equipped she bravely walked up to Jo's door. All of that bravery disappeared when she prepared to actually knock. She cleared her throat, straightened her shoulders and gave three firm knocks. A moment later the door opened a crack.

"What do you want?" Jo asked through the door.

"Hi Jo," Samantha said cheerfully.

Jo reluctantly opened her door. She peered at Samantha intently.

"What do you want?" she asked again, her voice barely hiding her animosity.

"Just to visit," Samantha explained and held up the box. "I brought muffins."

"Lovely," Jo narrowed her eyes. "Are you some kind of stalker?" she asked.

"No," Samantha said firmly and slipped the toe of her shoe in the crack of the door to keep Jo from closing it. "I just have a matter I need to discuss with you."

"A matter?" Jo asked, her eyes still narrowed.

"May I come in?" Samantha pressed, her smile still pleasant.

"Do I have a choice?" Jo countered and steadily stared at Samantha. "Now that you know my secret?"

"I'm not trying to cause any trouble for you, Jo," Samantha said. "Though we all know that our past can come back to haunt us."

"Sure, we all know that," Jo replied with a glare. She reluctantly stepped back and allowed Samantha to slip inside the door. When Jo closed the door behind her, Samantha was abruptly aware of the dangerous position she had put herself in. In all of the research Samantha had done on Jo there had never been one incident of violence involved in her crimes. But that did not mean that the woman was not capable of being violent if she wanted to be. If she thought it would benefit her to get rid of Samantha she might just do it.

"There's two other people that know I'm here," she abruptly blurted out. Jo took the box of muffins from her and set them down on the counter. She turned to face Samantha with a hint of a smile.

"I'm not going to murder you, Sam, if that's what you're thinking," she said with a short laugh. "You know that was never my style."

"I know," Samantha said nervously. "I guess I just don't know what to expect."

"Well, that makes two of us," Jo said as she folded her arms lithely across her slender stomach. "You have a lot of power over me right now, Samantha. You could make my life quite difficult if you wanted to. So, I think it's only fair that you be aware that I could make your life just as difficult, if I felt the need to."

"So, we're on the same footing," Samantha pointed out. "There's no reason why we can't have a civil discussion."

"Okay," Jo said, though she still eyed Samantha skeptically. "Then discuss."

"I want to thank you again for helping us out with finding the person who stole the watch," Samantha said.

"Oh, and here I thought you might apologize for not keeping my secret, like you promised," Jo said darkly. "And for accusing me of stealing."

Samantha cringed. "I am sorry about that," Samantha said as politely as she could. "But you can't blame me for suspecting you, considering your past."

Jo flicked her eyes away from Samantha with obvious irritation. Samantha continued to speak before Jo could decide to make her leave. "Anyway, James' death has been ruled a heart attack, but a few of us believe he might have been murdered."

"Oh?" Jo lofted a pencil thin black eyebrow. "What makes you think that?"

"We just have a suspicion that he might have been poisoned," Samantha explained. "The tox screen is pending."

"Who is we?" Jo asked with determination.

"Uh, just two friends," Samantha explained dismissively. She didn't think it would be a good idea to bring up Eddy's name.

"Their names?" Jo pressed. Her gaze was unrelenting. "I like to know who knows more about me than they should."

"Walter Right, and John Edwards," Samantha replied with a faint grimace. "They're not going to cause you any trouble either."

"So you say, I think Eddy would say different," Jo said and shook her head. "Not that your word should mean a lot to me, considering that you used to lie for a living."

"Lie for a living?" Samantha retorted. "What

are you talking about? I am a highly acclaimed journalist."

"You won all of those merits on the backs of your investigations, many of which were flawed," Jo countered. "Don't think I don't know a little bit about you Samantha Smith."

Samantha stared at her with surprise. She hadn't expected Jo to know much about her.

"Listen, I'm not here to argue with you about the honesty of our professions. I'm here to ask for your help," Samantha finally said in a wavering voice.

"I helped you once already," Jo snapped in return. "Why would I help you again?" she asked skeptically.

"We want to find out if Frank was involved in James' death. The only way we can know for sure is if we get some proof that the poisoning took place," Samantha explained. "We believe Frank is hiding the bottle of wine that he poisoned inside his villa. We want to break in and see if we can get the bottle."

"So, what does that have to do with me?" Jo shrugged.

"Well, I," Samantha hesitated and glanced at her shoes.

"Oh, I see," Jo nodded. "You don't want to break in yourselves, so you figured you'd recruit an expert."

"Is that so bad?" Samantha asked shyly. "I mean, it is what you do, isn't it?"

"I'm retired," Jo reminded her and sighed. "It would be a big risk for me you know. If I got caught I could be in trouble for a lot more than just breaking into a villa."

"I know," Samantha agreed. "I just don't know if we'll be able to do it ourselves. But, I guess it was a bad idea to ask. I'm sorry," she shook her head and started to turn away towards the door.

"Wait a minute," Jo said sharply. "I didn't say I wouldn't do it. I just said that it would be a risk. You could use it against me if you wanted to, since you know about my past."

"No," Samantha shook her head. "I wouldn't do that, Jo. You would be doing me a favor. It's not like we would be stealing anything valuable, it is for the sake of proving the truth. I would never get you in trouble with the law."

"You can say that now, yes," Jo replied. "But you can never know what the future might hold."

"That's true," Samantha agreed and looked into her eyes. "So, you'll help us?" she asked hopefully.

"I'll help you, Sam," Jo said with a small smile. "On one condition. I don't want to have to see or speak to that oaf of a man, Eddy. He's never going to believe that I have changed no matter what I do. I want a chance to live my life without always having to look over my shoulder. I don't think that's so wrong of me to want."

"Of course it isn't," Samantha agreed and smiled warmly at her. "Fine, then just you and I will go to Frank's. When do you want to go?"

Jo pursed her lips for a moment. She glanced at the clock on the wall, then looked back at

Samantha. "Tonight?" she suggested. "Do you think that you could get him out of the house?"

"I'm sure we can come up with something," Samantha agreed. She studied Jo for a long moment. She didn't know what she had expected from the woman, but she did know that this was not it. She seemed to be a kind person, who was willing to help others. It didn't compute to Samantha that she had once been a criminal.

"Are you just going to stare at me?" Jo asked. "Because that's rather creepy."

"Sorry," Samantha squeaked out. "I'll text you tonight."

"Fine, but we should have a code. Texts can be used against us if we get caught. Just say something like, dinner is ready, okay?"

"Good idea," Samantha nodded. "Thanks again, Jo."

"Don't thank me until we don't end up in jail," Jo said with a shake of her head. "I have a feeling that this is a really bad idea."

"It's just stealing a bottle of wine for the sake of justice. It's going to be fine," Samantha promised her. As she walked out of the villa she felt her heart racing. She had no idea if it would actually be fine.

*\*\**

When Samantha returned to the meeting point at the bench by the lake, she found only Walt waiting for her.

"Where's Eddy?" she asked before even greeting him. She shifted her gaze in the direction of Eddy's villa but did not see him walking up.

"I don't know if he's coming," Walt replied and shook his head slightly. "He was ranting this afternoon about crime and how we can't work with a known criminal."

"Did he say he wasn't coming?" Samantha asked with concern.

"No, he didn't outright say it, but I don't

know," Walt frowned and gazed out over the water. "He's right you know. We really shouldn't be working with someone who has a criminal past."

"So, Frank should just get away with murder?" Samantha demanded. "It was the poor man's birthday, Walt, and he was murdered in front of his son and all of his friends."

Walt sucked some air through his teeth and ran the palm of his hand back over the curve of his bare scalp.

"We don't even know if James was murdered. And if it is murder we don't know for sure that Frank is the one who did it. It still could have been James' son or anyone else for that matter. I've seen some good actors in my time. People that you would never think would be dirty, who are up to all kinds of scams, you can't always rely on a person's word that they wouldn't do something," he glanced over at Samantha. "You studied this woman, didn't you?" he asked.

"I think that you are missing the point,"

Samantha said grimly. "Jo's past isn't in question. She did her time, and now she's out. She's already helped us once, and now she's willing to help us again."

"Which makes her all the more suspicious, doesn't it?" Eddy asked from a few feet away from Samantha. Samantha jumped a little at the sound of his voice and turned to face him.

"Nice of you to show up," she muttered with disappointment.

"I'm allowed to have my misgivings," he replied, his expression detached.

"And now?" Samantha asked. "Are you on board with this?"

"You're going to go through with it whether I am or not, aren't you?" he asked as he took a step closer to her. "It doesn't really matter what my opinion is."

"Of course it matters," Samantha said gruffly. "But I think you're being awfully stubborn about Jo. I think if you could look past her history for just a second, you'd see that she's changed a lot."

"Prison can tame a criminal," Eddy said calmly. "But it does not change a criminal. She's still in the afterglow of experiencing freedom again. When she starts getting used to the idea, when she starts feeling entitled to be free again, then you'll see her true colors come out."

"I see it now," Samantha said quietly.

"You see what?" he asked as he studied her.

"I see why Jo hates us both. The way you're talking about her, is the same way I wrote about her," she shook her head with dismay. "It's easy to judge a criminal when you don't see them as a person, you just see them as their crime."

"Or maybe you're just getting soft, Samantha," Eddy said as he locked eyes with her. "Maybe you're falling for a con, and you're too eager for a friend to see Jo for who she truly is."

"I don't think so," Samantha replied, she was not intimidated by Eddy's intent stare. "Maybe you've just gotten so bitter that you don't know a good person when you meet them."

"A good person?" Eddy shook his head. "Jo is a criminal. She wouldn't think twice about turning against any of us. Sam," he sighed and wiped a hand across his face. "Look, I admire your desire to think this woman is somehow magically a good person, but I'm just trying to look out for you."

"Don't bother," Samantha said with a laugh. "I made it through so far without you looking over my shoulder, Eddy, and I'm sure I can make it through much more. It's happening tonight. I'll let you know what we find," Samantha spun on her heel and stalked away from the two men. She could hear them murmuring to each other behind her.

"You got her riled up," Walt said and scratched at the back of his neck.

"She's not making any sense," Eddy complained as he stared after Samantha. "How could she consider Jo a good person?"

"Well, she did help us with the watch," Walt

reminded him. "Besides, why does it matter so much to you? If Samantha wants to believe in the good in someone, let her," he sighed. "Too much of life is hard, Eddy, if she can still find something good, let her."

"I'm not arguing that point," Eddy frowned. "I'm trying to keep her from mistaking something deceitful for something good."

"And who is trying to keep you from mistaking a friend for an enemy?" Walt countered. He clapped his hand lightly against Eddy's back. "It's all about perspective, don't you think?"

"Not when it comes to crime," Eddy said gravely.

"Well, you keep trying to convince Samantha of that, and let me know how it works out," Walt chuckled. "I've never met a more stubborn woman."

"I just hope she isn't being more stubborn than smart about this," Eddy said with concern. He tugged his hat down lower on his head and sighed. "I'll have to keep an eye on things."

"Just don't get caught," Walt warned.

"I'll do my best," Eddy laughed.

# Chapter Fourteen

Samantha burst through the door of her villa, still annoyed with Eddy for the way he had spoken to her. She'd dealt with enough cops in her time to know when one was on a power trip. She closed the door behind her and walked over to her computer. She needed to find a reason for Frank to be out of his villa that evening. She searched for local events that she thought might interest him. Then she picked up her phone. She blocked her number from appearing on caller ID and dialed Frank's number. He picked up after two rings.

"This is Frank," he said.

"This is your lucky day, Frank," Samantha said in a slightly higher pitch than her normal voice. She made sure that she sounded very excited. "You've won two free tickets to a concert tonight."

"A concert?" he asked skeptically. "I didn't enter any contest."

"Are you a new resident of Sage Gardens?" Samantha asked cheerfully.

"Well yes," Frank replied.

"All new residents of Sage Gardens are entered into our contest. It's our way of helping new residents to get to know the area," Samantha explained. "Your tickets are completely free, but you have to be at the concert by seven tonight, or you will not get the free tickets."

"That's pretty short notice," Frank said with annoyance.

"Sorry, we had some technical issues and had been calling the previous resident's old number," Samantha explained swiftly. She had learned how to make up a good story in a short amount of time when investigating crimes for her articles.

"Oh?" Frank sighed. "Well, I guess it would be good for me to get out. Can you give me the address?"

"Sure," Samantha agreed and rattled off the address of one of the concerts that was taking place in town that night. She knew that by the time Frank got there and realized that there were no free tickets, Jo would be done searching his villa for the bottle of wine and the poison.

"All right, before seven, right?" he asked again.

"Yes, before seven. Don't be late," Samantha warned.

"I'll be there," Frank said, then he hung up the phone. Samantha hung up her phone and sighed with relief. She had been fairly certain that he wasn't going to believe her a few times during their conversation, but it seemed as if he had bought it in the end. She sent a text to Jo's phone.

*Can we get together around 7?*

Within seconds she received a text in response.

*Sounds good.*

Samantha smiled and then set her phone down on the table. She decided to spend the rest of her afternoon going through the articles she had written about Jo.

Samantha got so lost in the articles that she didn't realize it was nearly seven o'clock until her phone rang. She glanced at the clock and then snatched up the phone.

"Jo?" she asked.

"No," a voice replied. When Samantha recognized it, her heart skipped a beat. "It's Frank," he said. Samantha began to panic. Had he figured out that she was the one who had called him?

"Hi, Frank," she said carefully.

"Listen Samantha, I won two free tickets to a concert tonight. I was wondering if you might like to go along," Frank offered. "We'd have to leave in a few minutes though."

"Oh, I'm sorry, Frank, I can't tonight,"

Samantha stumbled out quickly. "I'm not feeling very well."

"All right then, I hope you feel better soon," Frank said before hanging up the phone. Samantha was startled by the call, but she was glad that Frank was actually planning on going to the concert.

She stepped out of her villa and locked the door behind her. She made her way slowly towards Frank's villa. Her slow movement paid off, as she was able to see him get in his car. She ducked behind a tree as he drove out of Sage Gardens. Samantha texted Jo a quick message.

*Dinner is ready*

Jo didn't answer right away. As the minutes ticked by, Samantha began to wonder if she was coming at all. She was starting to think that Eddy had been right and she had misjudged Jo. When it seemed like she wasn't coming she began to peek in Frank's windows.

"Thinking of a career change?" Jo asked from just behind her. Samantha nearly jumped out of her skin.

"I wasn't sure if you were coming," Samantha admitted.

"I'm here, aren't I?" Jo asked. She smoothed down the black turtle neck that she was wearing. "Any ideas where the wine bottle might be?" she asked.

"Maybe in the trashcan under the sink," Samantha replied.

"All right, let's get to it," Jo said with a nod. Her expression was impassive. She reached up to the edge of the black knit cap she was wearing and pulled it down. It covered her whole face aside from cut outs for her eyes and mouth.

"Are you sure that you can pull this off?" Samantha asked nervously as she looked into Jo's eyes. The deep nearly black spheres gazed back at Samantha with impatience.

"You know me so well, what do you think?" she asked.

Samantha smiled a little as she recalled the article she had just read over. Jo never made a mistake. That was why she was never caught.

"Jo, why did you turn yourself in?" Samantha suddenly asked her.

"You want to talk about that now?" Jo asked with disbelief.

"I'm just wondering," Samantha mumbled.

"Please, back off," Jo said sharply. Then she disappeared around the side of the villa. Once she was gone, Samantha ducked behind the next villa. She didn't want to be seen loitering. Her heart was racing. She wondered if Jo would make it out okay. She wondered what it meant to be encouraging a crime, and whether her morals were really as bad as Eddy had implied they might be. She didn't have much time to worry, as within five minutes Jo was walking casually back towards her. Her hands were empty.

"Couldn't you get in?" Samantha asked with disappointment.

"Yes, I got in," Jo replied. "Now, just start walking."

"Was it there?" Samantha asked breathlessly as she fell into step beside Jo. She matched Jo's casual pace.

"It was," Jo replied.

"Well, where is it?" Samantha asked impatiently.

"Would you please be quiet?" Jo demanded and shot a glare in her direction. "Do you want all of Sage Gardens to know what just happened?"

"Sorry," Samantha said darkly. She wanted to say more than that, but she knew that Jo had just gone out on a limb to help them, when she didn't have to.

"Let's go to your place," Jo said. "I'll give you the bottle there. I couldn't find any poison."

"No, not mine," Samantha said fearfully. She wasn't sure that she would handle the bottle correctly to preserve the evidence. "Let's take it to Eddy's place."

"Are you insane?" Jo asked sharply. "I will do no such thing."

"Don't worry, Eddy isn't going to give you a hard time," Samantha assured her. "He's just going to take care of the bottle so he can turn it in as evidence."

"I agreed to steal it, I didn't agree to turn it over to a cop," Jo snarled in return. "Unbelievable. Was all of this a set up? Was it your way of getting revenge on me?"

"No, of course not," Samantha shook her head quickly. "It's not like that at all. Eddy still has connections at the police department so he's hoping to turn the wine bottle over to the police in order to find out if it had poison in it and then prove that Frank was the one who poisoned James."

"I don't know," Jo said hesitantly.

"We're already here," Samantha said as she

paused in front of Eddy's villa. Eddy opened the door and stepped outside. Walt was just behind him. Both men stared at Jo. Jo shifted uncomfortably. She felt very exposed, especially with so many people gathered in one place.

"Let's get inside before someone notices the crowd," she said with a sigh. "We don't want to attract any attention."

Eddy watched her closely as he held open the door for both women to step inside. Once the door was shut behind them, he cleared his throat.

"Was it there?" he asked.

"Yes," Jo replied without looking in his direction. She pulled the wine bottle out of an inside pocket in her jacket and handed it over to him.

"What about the poison," Eddy asked.

"I couldn't find any," Jo said.

"Maybe he hid it," Eddy suggested.

"I'll just be going," Jo said and started to walk towards the door. Before she could reach the handle Eddy had his hand on her wrist. Jo gasped and looked over at him fearfully.

"Eddy, stop!" Samantha snapped out.

"I just wanted to say thank you," Eddy said as he met Jo's eyes. "It's nice to know that you still have it in you, to break into someone's home and steal from them."

"Seriously?" Jo shook his hand off her wrist. "This is the last time I help. I mean it, Sam," she said and stormed out of the villa.

"What was that?" Samantha demanded as she turned on Eddy.

"If she had really changed, she wouldn't have broken in," Eddy pointed out. He dropped the wine bottle into a plastic bag.

"Eddy, you're being ridiculous. She did this for us," Samantha said. "To help us solve a possible murder."

"I don't have time to argue about it right now, Samantha. I'm going to run this over to my contact. He's meeting me for dinner," he gestured to the door. "You two can find your own way out, I assume."

Then he brushed past them without the slightest hesitation.

# Chapter Fifteen

Eddy had observed the entire break in. Watching Jo work had made him feel such a strong urge to stop her and arrest her that it was hard for him to keep quiet. Luckily, neither woman had noticed him. At least he didn't think they did. He just couldn't stop seeing Jo shimmy in through the window and disappear into the darkness of the villa. She had a certain grace that he had never actually witnessed before. But to him it was anything but beautiful. It was criminal. As he drove to the diner where he was meeting his friend he tried to focus on the fact that hopefully soon Frank would be in jail, rather than Jo's actions. He parked in the diner parking lot and hurried inside. His friend was waiting for him at the table, with a plate of food already in front of him.

"You're late," he said as Eddy sat down across from him.

"Sorry," Eddy said. "It doesn't look like you

waited for me."

"There's more coming," he shrugged. Eddy swept his gaze over Vincent Dank. He was one of the worst detectives that Eddy had ever known. Eddy had taken him under his wing when he was a young detective and attempted to train him, but it didn't make much difference in the long run. All that mattered was that he was a connection that Eddy could use.

"I have the evidence," Eddy said and placed the bag with the wine bottle on the table. Dank regarded it for a moment and then looked up at Eddy.

"I'm telling you right now, Eddy, without a confession your suspect is going to get away with this murder," Dank said as he brushed a napkin across his lips. "You've got no evidence to connect him to the crime."

"But the bottle of wine," Eddy pressed, his eyes wide. "Can't you do something with it?" Eddy asked hopefully but he knew that the chance of it being used as evidence in James' murder was close to zero. He had hoped that Dank might run some tests and use it to investigate more. The waitress set down a plate of food in front of Eddy that Eddy hadn't even ordered. She knew him well enough to know what he liked.

"Maybe, if it could have been entered into evidence. But since you and your friends broke in and took it out of the man's house, there's no way for you to prove that it's the same bottle of wine that he gave to James as a gift. Meaning, you could have planted it if you wanted to. I can't even use it to justify looking into the case further," he raised an eyebrow. "I know you meant well, but that's why you have to follow procedure, Eddy."

"I know, I know," Eddy sighed and ran his palm along his face. That was one of the biggest problems he had with his captains when he was a detective. They always wanted the details, and he never took the time to follow the proper steps. "So, I guess it's a total loss," he said morosely.

"No, not necessarily," Dank said and pointed to his plate. "Are you going to eat that?" he asked.

Eddy glanced down at his uneaten french fries. He pushed the plate across the table to Dank.

"Go for it," he said. "Now, what were you saying about the murder?"

"Like I said, all you need is a confession, right?" he shrugged and chomped down on a french fry. "You believe he's guilty. This guy isn't exactly a career criminal. Just get him to admit to it. You're one of the best interrogators I know, Eddy," he chuckled a little before taking a sip of his soda.

"Thanks," Eddy nodded respectfully. His mind was already churning about the idea of interrogating Frank. "But I don't think that I'll be able to get him into a police station."

"You're a legend, Eddy, you don't need a police station," Dank said. He tapped his fingertip lightly on the side of his forehead. "Think outside the box."

His words ruffled Eddy, as they were the same words that Samantha had spoken to him recently.

"Is that a thing now?" he asked. "Is everybody supposed to think outside the box?"

"Well," Dank chomped down on another fry. "I guess it depends on the box."

Eddy smiled a little at that. "I guess you're right about that," he said with a nod. "Enjoy your meal, Dank. Thanks for the information," he said as he stood up from the table.

"Sorry I couldn't be more help," Dank said through a mouthful of french fry.

"You were plenty of help," Eddy assured him. He tossed a twenty down to cover their meals and then walked out of the restaurant. As he drove back towards Sage Gardens he thought about what Dank had said. If their only hope really was to get Frank to confess, then there were a few ways that he could make that happen. But he wasn't going to be able to do it alone.

\*\*\*

"Hello?" Samantha answered her phone, knowing that it was Eddy calling.

"Sam, we need to meet. See if you can get Walt to join us," Eddy said without greeting her.

"Okay, is there good news?" she asked hopefully. "Is your friend going to arrest Frank?"

"Not just yet," Eddy replied. "Let's meet at your place, okay?"

"Okay," Samantha agreed with a little more worry in her voice. When she hung up the phone she dialed Walt. He answered on the second ring.

"Walter speaking," he said.

"Walt, it's Samantha. I just got a call from Eddy and he wants us all to meet at my place," Samantha explained swiftly.

"Is Frank getting arrested?" Walt asked.

"Doesn't sound like it," Samantha replied with disappointment. "Let's just see what Eddy has to say when he gets here."

"All right," Walt replied. "I'll be there in a few minutes."

Samantha hung up her phone and then went about tidying up the few things that were a mess in her kitchen. She knew any kind of disorder would drive Walt nuts. She opened the fridge to see what she could offer them to drink. As she was rummaging around she heard a voice that made her skin crawl.

"Got any beer?" Frank asked from a few feet behind her.

Samantha slowly stood up and turned to face Frank. "What are you doing in my house?" she asked him, her voice strangled with fear.

"What am I doing in your house?" Frank asked with a low chuckle. "Well, let's see, Samantha, maybe I should have asked you that, when you broke into my house and stole from me."

"What are you talking about?" Samantha asked innocently. "Did someone break into your villa?"

"Oh yes, plead ignorance," he shook his head and stepped further into the kitchen. "Doesn't matter if you want to pretend you have no idea what I'm talking about. I know it was you. You're the only one who would have thought about the wine bottle in my trashcan. What I don't understand is why you would steal my trash?" he asked dismissively.

"I didn't steal any trash from you," Samantha said crossly. "Maybe it got stuck behind that malfunctioning waste bin of yours."

"Ha, sure," Frank nodded and leaned back against the counter beside her. "Only, I know that you broke in or made someone else do it. I know that you stole from me, so all of this nonsense is pointless. Don't you think?"

"I don't have a clue what you're rambling on about, Frank. To be honest I'm not comfortable with you being in my house, especially with the way you are talking. I think you should leave, before I have to call security," Samantha warned him.

"Oh?" he laughed again. "Please do. Let's call security and let them know that you broke into my villa. I'm sure that they would be very interested in that."

Samantha shifted uncomfortably. She wasn't sure if he had any real proof that they had broken into his villa. But if he did and she called security, then they would be in a lot of trouble.

"Just go, Frank," she said sternly.

"I'm not going anywhere," Frank said in return. His eyes were shining with an emotion that Samantha couldn't quite grasp. It was something between dominance and drunkenness. She felt her stomach twist as she wondered exactly what he intended to do to her. "I want to know why you were in my house," he bit out each word as he leaned close to her.

"I wasn't," she sputtered out.

"You must have been," he argued. "Because when I left the house, the wine bottle was in the trash. When I came back, it was gone. Does that make sense to you, Samantha?"

"Maybe you just forgot that you put the trash

out," she suggested fearfully.

"I didn't put the trash out," he growled. "The bag was still in the trashcan. I'll give you one more chance, Samantha," he said and placed his hand firmly on her shoulder so that she was pinned back against the counter. "Why were you in my house?" he demanded.

Samantha was terrified as she looked into his eyes. She had never felt so frightened before, and the certainty that he had been responsible for James' death made it even worse. She was trembling too much to speak.

"Get your dirty hands off her," Eddy growled from the doorway of the kitchen.

Frank was clearly startled by his presence. He abruptly let go of Samantha and turned around to face Eddy. "We were just having a conversation, my friend. No need to be jealous."

"Jealous?" Eddy snapped. "Since when does a conversation involve holding someone hostage?"

"Look, I just had some business to discuss

with her," Frank insisted as if everything was casual. "I don't want any trouble with you, Eddy. I just had a few questions for Samantha."

"Frank thinks I broke into his villa," Samantha said quickly. She looked into Eddy's eyes with a mixture of gratitude and lingering fear.

"Frank knows you did," Frank corrected her with a slight glare. When he looked back at Eddy he was not the least bit intimidated by his presence. "Do you mind? This really is a private conversation."

"I'm not going anywhere," Eddy said darkly. "I think it's time for you to leave, Frank."

"Oh, do you?" Frank shook his head and leaned back against the kitchen counter. "I think it's time we got a few things straight."

"Fine," Eddy said as he moved over in front of Samantha. "Then maybe you would like to start by telling me why after over thirty years you decided to get your revenge on James?"

Frank was silenced by Eddy's question. He stared at him with a hint of panic in his eyes.

"James had a heart attack," Frank finally said calmly. "It was unfortunate and unexpected, but it was just a heart attack. Are you saying that somehow I'm responsible for his heart attack?"

"It must have been upsetting for him to see you," Eddy suggested and lightly guided Samantha to step back from the conversation. Samantha lingered close to Eddy. Not only did she not feel the need to be protected, she also didn't want to miss a word of the conversation that was unfolding.

"For him to see me?" Frank asked with a sharp chuckle.

"With your past," Samantha piped up from behind Eddy. Eddy shot her a glare of warning over his shoulder when she spoke up. Samantha pretended not to notice.

"I think he was surprised," Frank said solemnly. "What man wouldn't be surprised when he was confronted with the person whose life he ruined?"

"It was a long time ago," Eddy pointed out.

"Not really," Frank shrugged a little. "For me it was every day. You see, I actually loved my wife," he smiled. "A lot of men say that, don't they?" he shrugged. "They love their wives, if someone asks them, if it's their anniversary, if their wife should get sick, or unexpectedly pass away. But not too many men mean it. I guess there are different kinds of love. I've loved women since my wife, at least I told them I did. But I really only enjoyed their company. Elena, I was head over heels in love with. She was the one, my one and only. We were supposed to have children together, grow old together," he shook his head slowly. "Do you know what that's like? I couldn't even imagine having a child with anyone else, or spending my life with someone else. It wasn't a choice that I could make, it was a necessity. So yes, he came along and ruined that. He seduced her with his money, he made her think that she could have a better life with him."

"That must have been incredibly difficult for you," Samantha supplied quietly.

"There isn't a word for the emotions I experienced," Frank admitted. "But pure hatred, no matter how deserved it is, doesn't cause a person to have a heart attack, does it?" he asked. "So, why are you implying that I am responsible for James' death?"

"You're right, hatred alone doesn't cause a heart attack, but there are some poisons that can mimic a heart attack," Eddy pointed out as he studied the man before him and did his best to shield Samantha behind him, despite her attempts to avoid him.

"Poison?" Frank asked and shook his head. "Now, you've really lost it pal. He died of a heart attack."

"That's not necessarily true," Samantha replied. "The medical examiner is investigating the possibility that James was poisoned."

"Oh?" Frank asked and stood up from the counter. "I didn't know that."

"We think maybe something he ate or drank, maybe one of his gifts, was laced with poison," Eddy explained as he watched Frank closely.

"Can't say the jerk didn't deserve it," Frank glowered. "I guess someone decided to do me a favor."

"Is that how you're going to play this, Frank?" Eddy demanded as he moved away from Samantha and towards Frank. "You're going to pin your actions on someone else?"

"I had nothing to do with James' death," Frank shook his head. "I was at the party celebrating his birthday. I even talked to Samantha there, didn't I Samantha?"

"Some," Samantha nodded.

"And you really think I'm capable of murder?" Frank questioned. He sought Samantha's eyes intently.

"I think that anyone is capable of anything when they are pushed past their breaking point," Samantha explained in return.

"Well, that may be, but there is no way you can prove that I killed James," Frank said and offered a subtle smirk. "I'm innocent."

"We have the wine bottle," Samantha blurted out.

"Oh, do you?" Frank asked with fury in his eyes. "As if I didn't already know that."

"Then you aren't denying what you did?" Eddy asked and slipped his hand into his pocket. He set his cell phone to record.

"What I did?" Frank repeated. "I bought my old friend, who I clearly forgave, a bottle of his favorite wine. What's so wrong with that?"

"You poisoned the wine," Samantha accused.

"I did no such thing," Frank argued. His eyes were wide with shock.

"If you didn't poison the wine then why did you sneak into James' room to steal the remainder of the bottle?" Eddy asked.

"I took my gift back," Frank said with a slight shrug. "It wasn't really stealing. I knew that James wasn't going to finish the bottle if he was dead. It was an expensive bottle of wine. I'm not stupid. I was sure the staff around here would pick James' room clean of anything valuable. So, I went and got the bottle before anyone could take it. That wasn't really a crime."

Eddy stared hard at the man before him. His heart was pounding. It was suddenly becoming very clear to him that Frank was going to get away with murder. Without the bottle to enter as evidence, there was only going to be one way to bring the man to justice. He would have to confess.

"You think you're really slick, don't you?" Eddy demanded as he pointedly stepped between Frank and Samantha again. Samantha watched Eddy's movements closely as she wondered exactly what he was up to.

"I think that you're really trying to play detective," Frank replied with a faint smile on his lips. "You want to make this interesting, when it's not. It's a simple heart attack. James finally paid for all of his sins. Just because you want there to be a crime here, so that you can fill your boring endless days of retirement with something fun, that doesn't mean that there is actually a crime."

"I know differently," Eddy bit out his words. "I know what you have done, Frank, and I am not about to allow you to get away with it."

"Oh? Tough one are you?" Frank shook his head. "You can't do anything to me that hasn't already been done."

Eddy glanced briefly over at Samantha who was watching him closely. She seemed to be attempting to predict what his next move was going to be. Eddy knew what it would be, but he wasn't sure if Samantha would go along with it. It was a very risky move, but one that he had already decided had to happen.

"Let's find out," Eddy said and crossed the distance between them.

"Watch it!" Frank growled and lunged for the back door of the villa. "I'll just be on my way."

"I don't think so," Eddy growled and grabbed Frank by the crook of his arm. He spun him back around to face him before he could get out through the back door.

"What do you think you're doing?" Frank shouted and glared into Eddy's eyes.

"Samantha, lock the door," Eddy said sternly. Samantha was frozen as she watched the two men interact. She had no idea how to react to such a dangerous and escalating situation.

"Sam!" Eddy said again in a more commanding tone. Samantha jumped and moved quickly to the back door. Her fingers trembled as she locked the door.

"Eddy," she began to say when she turned back to face him.

"In here," Eddy said and shoved Frank towards the small spare room in Samantha's villa. Samantha used it as office space for her writing. It was pretty bare aside from a wooden desk and chair as well as her desktop computer.

"Let go of me!" Frank demanded and struggled with Eddy. Eddy had handled enough criminals to defend himself. He easily shoved Frank into the room. Samantha started to follow him into the room. She was still uncertain of what exactly to do. Eddy took care of that uncertainty by closing the door behind him before she could enter.

"Eddy!" Samantha gasped and knocked on the door.

"We just need a few minutes, Sam," Eddy said. She heard the lock click on the door. Samantha's eyes widened with fear. She wondered what Eddy was going to do to Frank in the room alone. As she started to panic she reached for her phone. Her fingers were still trembling as she dialed Walt's number.

"Hello?" Walt asked.

"Walt, I think Eddy has lost it," Samantha said fearfully into the phone.

"What? Why?" Walt asked.

"He's got Frank locked in my office and he won't let me in," Samantha gulped her words out. She was trying to keep her voice low as she didn't want Eddy to know that she was calling Walt.

"What was Frank doing at your place?" Walt asked with confusion.

"He just let himself in," Samantha replied. "But now Eddy has him trapped, and I'm not sure what he's going to do to Frank."

"Okay, okay, just take a deep breath, Samantha," Walt instructed her. "Eddy might be acting like he's going to hurt Frank, but I doubt he really will. Remember, he's a professional."

"He's retired, Walt!" Samantha reminded him impatiently. "What if he decides to cross the line?"

"This is all because the police aren't going to use the wine bottle as evidence or as justification for further investigations," Walt sighed. "Eddy must think that Frank is going to get away with murder. All right, I'll be right over," he said before hanging up the phone. Samantha hung up the phone and shoved it back into her pocket. She began pacing back and forth outside the office door.

# Chapter Sixteen

Eddy grabbed the wooden office chair and slid it across the laminate floor. He pushed it up against the wall of the room. Then he tugged down the shade until the room became dim.

"You are going to be arrested for this you know?" Frank demanded. "This is insane!"

In the shadows of the room it was quite clear that Eddy was an intimidating presence. He had the brim of his hat pulled down low to cast an even thicker shadow over his face. His eyes were narrowed sharply, the glint of his gaze shimmering in what little light existed in the small room.

"We're just going to continue our discussion," Eddy explained.

"What are you thinking?" Frank demanded with increasing animosity. "You can't lock me in here. I haven't done anything wrong. You are going to pay for this!"

"I'm going to pay for it?" Eddy asked with a chuckle. "I don't think so, Frank. Why don't you just tell me, why did you kill James?"

"I didn't kill anyone," Frank shot back and then glared at Eddy. "I don't care who you think you used to be, you can't hold me here like this. You're basically kidnapping me."

"I'm having a conversation, Frank," Eddy replied and lifted his hat off his head. He ran his hand back over his thinning brown hair and then smiled at Frank. "Just two neighbors, chatting it up a bit."

"The door is locked," Frank reminded him flatly. "Neighbors don't usually lock each other up."

"Oh, that lock, Samantha has reported it to management a few times, but they haven't gotten around to fixing it yet. It's always acting up. Sometimes you can't lock it, sometimes you can't unlock it. So, to pass the time, we're just having a conversation."

"I'm not having any conversation with you,"

Frank shot back. "I don't know what you are thinking, but whatever it is you should know that you have the wrong man."

"You know something, Frank, in my career as a detective I have to say that I was wrong many times. Sometimes I was wrong about the way I handled things. Sometimes I was wrong about the motive behind a crime. But one thing I never got wrong, was the suspect," he narrowed his eyes. "I have never gotten the wrong man."

"Then you must be getting rusty, because you got the wrong one this time," Frank shot back and tried to stand up from the chair. Eddy easily pushed him back down.

"No, you're not going anywhere. I want to talk to you about the man you used to be," Eddy explained.

"What?" Frank stared up at him with disbelief. "You don't know anything about me."

"I think I know a lot more than you think I do," Eddy corrected him. "I think once, you were a romantic."

"A romantic?" Frank asked sharply. "Would you stop with this nonsense and let me go!"

"You fell in love. Not just with a woman, but with the love of your life. You married her, and you were ready to start the rest of your life with her. It never even entered your mind that your lovely lady wasn't as happy as she was pretending to be," Eddy smirked arrogantly.

"No, that's not what happened," Frank growled. "I was busy with work. I wanted to make enough so that we could buy the bigger house that she wanted. She didn't want to have any kids until we had a larger space. So, I took on extra hours and shifts to try to build up a solid savings account for us."

"Very noble of you," Eddy said with a slight nod.

"It's what a man does," Frank said darkly. "It's what he does when he starts a family. He takes care of that family, he provides for that family."

"That's all well and good, but it's not what every man does, is it?" Eddy asked and raised an eyebrow. "While you were out working so hard, your wife was sitting at home alone. She was wondering why she had even gotten married if her husband was only going to neglect her."

"No!" Frank tried to stand up again. Eddy shoved him firmly back down into the chair.

"Sit," he muttered. Frank was too lost in his emotion to even argue.

"Yes, I was working a lot, but she loved me for it. She would tell me how hard I worked, and what a good man I was," Frank insisted. "At least, at first she would. Then James started coming around more often. I was working so hard, so when things needed to be fixed in the house, I would ask James if he could stop over and take a look at it for me."

"James, your best friend," Eddy said softly. "Sometimes friendship can be even stronger than having a brother."

"James was my brother," Frank admitted sadly. "In my mind anyway."

"But your wife started to notice that your brother was around and interested in her," Eddy suggested. He wanted to keep Frank bristled and on edge.

"No," Frank growled again. "You're wrong. She loved me. But James had this way with women. IIe could get them to do anything hc wanted. He seduced her."

"You think he forced her?" Eddy asked with a slight laugh. "Trust me, Frank, a woman doesn't turn around and marry a man who attacks her."

"I didn't say he forced her," Frank said through gritted teeth. "I said he seduced her. He manipulated her and convinced her that she wanted to be with him, not with me."

"I bet that was upsetting," Eddy suggested in a murmur.

"It was!" Frank shouted. "Of course it was!"

"Even more upsetting was finding out that she never loved you in the first place, wasn't it, Frank?" Eddy asked with feigned sympathy.

"What was it that set you off, Frank? After all these years? Did you finally realize that it was James she loved all along?"

"No, no, no," Frank shook his head quickly. "It was all lies, all of it."

"What did Elena tell you, Frank?" Eddy asked in a whisper. "How did she confess it?"

Frank squeezed his eyes shut tight and groaned. "I wish I'd never seen that damn letter."

"What letter?" Eddy demanded. "What did the letter say, Frank?"

"Elena knew she was going to die. She was terminally ill. So, she thought she'd get right with the world before she passed. She wrote letters to everyone she thought she had wronged. She sent me one. It said that she had married me because she thought I would make a good husband and father, and that the passion would come later. But it never did. She only had passion for," he growled and couldn't finish his sentence.

"For James," Eddy supplied. "So, after all this

time of believing that James had stolen her from you, you had to face the fact that she just had stronger feelings for James than you. Is that why you poisoned him, Frank?"

"When I saw him again," Frank muttered without answering Eddy's question. "When I looked into his eyes and I realized that he was the man that had ruined my life, I couldn't believe it."

"So, you knew that James lived here?" Eddy pressed.

"I didn't, not until after I moved in. I saw him walking by, he didn't see me. I started to think about the things I would do to him if I could," Frank admitted. "He took everything from me. But they were just fantasies. I wasn't going to do anything."

"Fantasies that led you to lacing a bottle of wine with poison?" Eddy prompted.

"It wasn't like that," Frank moaned and hung his head. "It wasn't like I walked up to him and shot him. It wasn't murder."

"How is killing a man, poisoning him, not murder?" Eddy demanded. "Don't lie to me, Frank!"

Frank stepped back from the sheer volume of Eddy's voice.

Outside the office, Samantha heard the shout. She cringed at the sound of it. Her front door swung open and Walt came walking in with a scowl.

"Is that Eddy I just heard?" he asked.

"Yes," Samantha gasped out. "I don't know what he's doing in there, but I've never heard him so angry before."

"He's yelling loud enough for the entire block to hear," Walt said with concern.

"What do you think we should do?" Samantha asked. She was beside herself with worry. Her mind was spinning as she considered calling the police, but she didn't want Eddy to be punished for trying to do what they had all set out to do, capture a murderer.

# Chapter Seventeen

Eddy leaned close to Frank, his eyes boring into the other man's. "I'm not going anywhere until you tell me what really happened, Frank."

"All right fine," Frank muttered and wiped a hand across his forehead. "I'm not lying though. I'm not a murderer."

"Yet, you just admitted to poisoning James," Eddy pointed out and slid his hand into his pocket to make sure that his phone was still recording.

"Yes," Frank stared hard at his own palms. "Sometimes things happen in life that take a good man, and turn him into a murderer"

"All those years of being a good man do not make up for the murderer that you became," Eddy said sternly. "The only way you can be a good man again is if you tell the truth. You made a mistake. You let your emotions take over. After the letter you received from Elena and being faced with James again, it's understandable that you couldn't control yourself," Eddy sighed and shook his head. "What I don't understand is how did you do it?'

"It was the strangest thing. It was like everything just fell into place. I was helping the committee set up. I found out who the party was for. I decided rather than being petty I would buy James a bottle of his favorite wine. I intended to kill him with kindness. When I got the bottle of wine, I remembered the times we had shared together. We were best friends all through high school. We went to college together. We shared that wine on so many occasions. The only time I really thought everything was right with the world was when James was by my side, and then," he paused and looked up at Eddy tearfully. "And then all I could think about was finding him with Elena. They didn't even try to hide it," he shook his head. "When I walked in, James just shrugged and told me it was good that I knew and that we could all move on.  As if I was supposed to just move on from something as upsetting as that,"

Frank's eyes widened. "How could I ever move on from that?"

"So, you relived the entire scene in your mind," Eddy urged him to continue.

"It was more than that," Frank admitted. "It was all I could think about. Over and over in my mind. I tried to push it out of my head. I tried not to think about it. But I couldn't stop it. Some of the fantasies I had about how I would kill him if I could began to surface again as well. One was to poison his food. Then I was in the shop buying the wine and suddenly I thought about poisoning it. As soon as I thought about it, I remembered the cyanide I kept from my days in the jewelry business."

"That was a damaging thought," Eddy said softly. He didn't want to do anything to stop the flow of Frank's confession.

"It was just a thought," Frank said with a sigh. "I wasn't going to use it. It was just like a joke. But then on the drive home, I just kept thinking about it. All of a sudden it began to make sense. James didn't really deserve to live. He had stolen my life. He had gotten to live all of the best parts that I was supposed to live, so it was only fair that I end it. It wasn't murder. It was balancing the fates."

"But that wasn't your decision to make, Frank," Eddy reminded him darkly. "And a bottle of wine didn't kill James. The poison that you put inside it did. What if James had decided to share it with everyone at the party?"

"Like I said, I didn't think about it," Frank sighed. "I just did it. I didn't even know if it would kill him or just make him sick. I certainly didn't expect it to have such a strong effect so quickly. When James died, it didn't even feel real to me. I didn't think that it could really be my fault. When it started to dawn on me I panicked. I was afraid someone else would drink what was left of the wine, that's why I stole it," he shook his head and gazed down at his own hands. "I didn't really kill him, it just happened."

"No, you poisoned the bottle of wine and gave it to a man who was once your best friend to drink.

You killed him. It was your way of getting even," Eddy said sharply.

"If he had never done what he did, then it never would have happened," Frank said harshly. "It doesn't matter anyway, you can't prove any of this."

Eddy stared at him for a moment, then he turned away from Frank. He unlocked the door and pulled it open.

"Samantha," Eddy said. Samantha and Walt turned around quickly to face Eddy. "Call the police."

"Are you sure?" Samantha asked nervously.

"We have everything we need," Eddy said with confidence and started to reach into his pocket for his phone. As he was sliding his hand into his pocket, Frank suddenly grabbed his shoulders from behind him. He yanked Eddy back into the room, and slammed the door shut.

"Eddy!" Samantha gasped and jerked at the handle of the door. It wouldn't budge. She turned towards Walt who was already on the phone calling the police. Frank shoved Eddy into the wall beside the computer table. Eddy felt his shoulder hit the wall hard and cried out in pain. It had been a long time since he was on the receiving end of violence and it didn't help that his body was much older. Frank shoved his hand into Eddy's pocket and grabbed his cell phone.

"Did you really think I didn't know what all of this was about?" Frank demanded. "Just how stupid do you think I am?"

"I don't know what you mean," Eddy growled in return and tried to wriggle out of his grasp.

"I knew you were recording me," Frank held up Eddy's phone in front of his face. "You thought you had me, but without this you have nothing." He shoved Eddy down into the same wooden chair that he had been sitting in. Then he opened the window behind him and threw the cell phone out through it. "Now, what do you have?" he asked as he turned back to face Eddy. "Nothing. But do you know what I have?" he smiled darkly. "I have a crazy man locking me up and harassing me. You're going to jail, Eddy, maybe you'll see some old friends there."

Eddy's heart sank as he heard the sirens outside. The police were arriving which meant that he had to do something or he risked being arrested.

"That's right," Frank said. "You should have just left it alone. James had a heart attack. He deserved to die. I didn't deserve anything that he did to me. Now you're going to get what you deserve," Frank laughed a little. There was pounding on the door.

"Eddy?" Samantha called through the door. "The police are here."

"Oh, good," Frank said and unlocked the door. He opened it up. Then he glanced back at Eddy with a slight smile. "I think they're going to be looking for you."

"Come in, he's in the back room," Walt said as he opened the front door. Two police officers walked into Samantha's villa with some confusion.

"We got a call about a murder?" the first officer asked.

"Well yes, but the murder didn't happen today," Samantha explained. "The killer is right here," she pointed to Frank who was just stepping out of the back room.

"Is that what he has you believing?" Frank asked and shook his head. "Officers, there is a mentally ill man here, he has taken me hostage and he's been ranting the entire time. He's really lost his mind."

"I haven't lost anything," Eddy said sternly as he stepped out of the room. "I am a retired police detective, and I know this man is guilty of murder."

"You do?" the first officer asked and looked at Eddy skeptically. "Do you have any proof of that, Sir?"

"Well, I did," Eddy frowned. "I had a recording of his confession but he threw it out the window. I'm sure the phone is still there, we'll just have to look for it."

"Do you hear this insanity?" Frank demanded and shook his head. "He thinks I killed someone, a resident here who recently died of a heart attack. I guess that he is having a hard time dealing with the loss."

"All right, Sir, you're going to have to come with us," the first officer said and began moving towards Eddy.

"No!" Samantha gasped out. "You can't do that, he didn't do anything wrong!"

"She's just as crazy," Frank sighed.

Suddenly, Frank's voice filled the room, but it was not coming from his mouth.

"Like I said, I didn't think about it, I just did it."

"Where is that coming from?" Frank demanded. He was suddenly irate, causing the second officer to close in on him.

"There's a lot more to hear," Jo said as she

stepped fully into the villa. "Should I let it keep playing?" she asked. She was doing her best not to look directly at the police officers.

"That's my phone," Eddy said with a mixture of relief and shock. "Everything you need is on there," Eddy insisted.

"All right, let's just get all of this sorted out," the first officer said with a sigh. "You, you, and you," he pointed at Frank, then Eddy, then Jo. "You're all coming down to the station with me."

"No," Jo said and started to back out of the villa.

"She had nothing to do with this," Eddy said. "She must have been walking by when Frank threw my phone out the window."

The two officers looked at each other and then nodded. "All right then."

Jo looked into Eddy's eyes with relief.

"Eddy, are you going to be okay?" Samantha asked. "Do you want me to come with you?"

"I'll be fine," Eddy assured her. As he walked

out with the officers, he glanced over at Jo.

"Thank you," he whispered to her. Jo lowered her eyes.

# Chapter Eighteen

By the next morning Frank was in jail. Eddy was back at Sage Gardens, standing beside Samantha. Owen had called Mike the moment he heard the truth from Eddy. Mike was just leaving after his conversation with Owen.

"It's a terrible shame," Samantha said in a murmur as she watched Mike's car pulling out of the parking lot.

"Hmm?" Eddy asked as he looked over at her.

"His son was finally able to forgive him for what he had done in the past, but then Frank came along and took his revenge," she sighed and shook her head. "I know that there is never an excuse for murder, Eddy, but I can't begin to imagine how betrayed Frank must have felt when he discovered James and his wife together."

"And then to have to live with that betrayal for so many years," Eddy agreed solemnly. "Poor James had his own regrets, but apologies aren't always enough."

"Have you ever had your heart broken like that?" she asked curiously and offered him a sidelong glance.

"Oh, no you don't," Eddy said with a playful scowl. "I'm not falling into that trap."

"What trap?" she asked. "It's an honest question."

"An honest question that there is no right answer to," he clarified. "I could say, no I've never felt that way before, and you'll think I'm lying, or that I'm too cold hearted to have ever been in love. I could say yes, I've been heart broken, so badly that I could barely bring myself to get out of bed in the morning, then you will have a thousand questions about that. Nope, it's a deep hole that I'm not falling into, Samantha."

"You know something, Eddy?" Samantha asked with an exaggerated sigh.

"What?" he asked in return and met her eyes.

"It was just a simple question. What is it with men? They can't ever answer, just yes or no," she smiled slyly at him.

"Clever," he chuckled and slid an arm around her shoulders to give her a soft squeeze. "Let's go see if Walt has survived all of this. I'm sure he's already missing us."

"Somehow, I doubt that," Samantha laughed. "He's probably busy putting everything back into place that we got out of order during our visit."

"Yes, that does seem highly likely," he agreed as they began to walk towards Walt's villa. Samantha caught sight of Jo walking towards the mailboxes. She had her eyes trained to the ground. Samantha knew that she could just pretend that she didn't see her. That they could go right back to pretending they had no idea who each other was. But something about the way she didn't bother to look up left Samantha aching with sympathy for her. After all she had done to help them, Samantha simply couldn't fathom the idea of not speaking to her again.

"Hey Jo," she called out and raised her hand in a wave. Jo glanced up, obviously annoyed and reluctantly waved back to Samantha.

"What are you doing?" Eddy asked through gritted teeth.

"I'm saying hello to a friend of mine," Samantha replied stubbornly.

"Some friend," Eddy said gruffly.

"She helped you by getting the tape," Samantha pointed out.

"It doesn't change what she did in the past," he replied. His gaze lingered on Jo for a long moment. "Let's go," he said and steered Samantha away from Jo. Jo had already started to walk to the mailboxes again. Samantha shrugged Eddy's arm off her shoulder and looked up at him.

"She's paid her debt, if I want to be friends with her, then I will," she said sternly.

"If that's a risk you really want to take, I can't stop you," Eddy replied. "I just hope that she proves to be as rehabilitated as you seem to think she is."

"I guess time will tell," Samantha replied. As

they continued towards Walt's villa, Sage Gardens grew still with the quiet of evening. Everyone had forgotten about the heart attack that had turned out to be murder. They were all tuned into their televisions, card games, or novels. But there were four people who lived in Sage Gardens that would never forget.

The End

# More Cozy Mysteries by Cindy Bell

## Dune House Cozy Mysteries

Seaside Secrets

Boats and Bad Guys

Treasured History

Hidden Hideaways

Dodgy Dealings

## Heavenly Highland Inn Cozy Mysteries

Murdering the Roses

Dead in the Daisies

Killing the Carnations

Drowning the Daffodils

Suffocating the Sunflowers

Books, Bullets and Blooms

A Deadly serious Gardening Contest

A Bridal Bouquet and a Body

## Wendy the Wedding Planner Cozy Mysteries

Matrimony, Money and Murder

Chefs, Ceremonies and Crimes

Knives and Nuptials

## Bekki the Beautician Cozy Mysteries

Hairspray and Homicide

A Dyed Blonde and a Dead Body

Mascara and Murder

Pageant and Poison

Conditioner and a Corpse

Mistletoe, Makeup and Murder

Hairpin, Hair Dryer and Homicide

Blush, a Bride and a Body

Shampoo and a Stiff

Cosmetics, a Cruise and a Killer

Lipstick, a Long Iron and Lifeless

Camping, Concealer and Criminals